Praise for Edy Poppy

"Poised, bold and intelligent, *Anatomy. Monotony.* is an enthralling story of wildly experimental lives, in which both the pains and the gains of casting aside sexual norms are unsparingly examined."
—Rob Doyle, author of *Here are the Young Men*

"There is a riveting, devil-may-care impulse in Poppy's use of language and in her perspective. She explores mood nuances and emotional variations in the magnetic field between euphoric highs and pathetic lows."
—Nora Simonhjell, *Morgenbladet*

"*Coming. Apart.* is a knife-edge book that confirms that women have taken over the writing of interesting short stories." —Vidar Kvalshaug, *Aftenposten*

"The words flow with velvety smoothness, softly and lightly in spite of their gravity. Delightful!" —Anita Hartviksen Ravn, *Rana Blad*

"Edy Poppy's *Anatomy. Monotony* is a devilish hybrid. Part autofiction, part literary, cinematic, and musical dance of allusions, and part chronicle of the mute body's aches and pains and lusts and needs, the novel deftly hits its notes, high and low, to create a symphonic work of tragicomedy."
—Siri Hustvedt, author of *The Summer Without Men*

"A female, sexually free *Catcher in the Rye*." —Mike S. Ryan, producer of *Junebug*

"There's something both effortless and seductively bold about Edy Poppy's *Iggy*. The novel offers wit, steaming sex and several sad, but true acknowledgements. Words like 'shameless' and 'without boundaries' can be added as well."—Turid Larsen, *Dagsavisen*

Other Books by Edy Poppy Available in English Translation

Anatomy. Monotony.

Coming. Apart.

by
Edy Poppy

translated by
May-Brit Akerholt

DALKEY ARCHIVE PRESS
Dallas, TX / Rochester, NY

Deep Vellum | Dalkey Archive Press
3000 Commerce Street, Dallas, Texas 75226
www.dalkeyarchive.com

Deep Vellum is a 501c3 nonprofit literary arts organization founded in 2013
with the mission to bring the world into conversation through literature.

Originally published in Norwegian as Sammen. Brudd.
by Gyldendal Norsk Forlag AS., Oslo, Norway, 2011

First English edition, 2025

Support for this publication has been provided in part by grants from the National Endowment for the Arts, the Texas Commission on the Arts, the City of Dallas Office of Arts and Culture, the Communities Foundation of Texas, and the Addy Foundation.

THE ADDY
FOUNDATION

This translation has been published with the financial support of NORLA

Library of Congress Cataloging-in-Publication Data

Names: Poppy, Edy, 1975- author. | Akerholt, May-Brit, translator. Title: Coming, apart / by Edy Poppy ; translated by May-Brit Akerholt. Other titles: Sammen, brudd. English Description: Dallas, TX : Dalkey Archive Press, 2025. Identifiers: LCCN 2025007679 (print) | LCCN 2025007680 (ebook) | ISBN 9781628976281 (trade paperback) | ISBN 9781628976298 (ebook) Subjects: LCGFT: Short stories. Classification: LCC PT8952.26.O64 S3613 2025 (print) | LCC PT8952.26.O64 (ebook) | DDC 839.823/8--dc23/eng/20250227 LC record available at https://lccn.loc.gov/2025007679
LC ebook record available at https://lccn.loc.gov/2025007680
Cover art and design by Daniel Benneworth-Gray
Interior design and typeset by Douglas Suttle
Printed in the United States of America

Coming.
Apart.

Cyril and Ragnhild
(7 November 1992–13 June 2008)

Table of Contents

THE LAST SHORT STORY

Dear editor,

I know you're waiting for my last short story, but unfortunately, I have to disappoint you. It's taken me more than five years to write this collection, but now that it'll soon be finished, I'm wondering if I should throw the whole piece of crap in the bin and start something new. A novel.

I feel I haven't been honest enough in my short stories. Not courageous enough either. I've tried to write about the idea of coming apart in all sorts of different ways—a kind of encyclopedia of misery, if you like. I've seen myself crying in the mirror, thinking it was genuine. That it was literature. But I've only scratched the surface, without really meeting my own eyes, or those of the reader, for that matter.

"The truth is just a seed that fiction can grow from," I've told journalists. Or: "You can only reach the truth via lies." It's just a conceit, all of it. I've hidden behind the language, behind lovely formulations. Now I'm longing for an ugly, unpretentious form of writing. Sentences you don't know how to adhere to.

When I wrote *Anatomy. Monotony.*, I wanted Ragnhild to be a sympathetic character: the reader should like her because she represented me. Of course, I gave her a few flaws, but I didn't go far enough—not by a long shot. I was vain, chickened out. Now I want to write until I blush. Because I believe that's where the most interesting writing, the most challenging formulations, are hiding: in the total degradation.

I don't want to write about Ragnhild anymore. She doesn't represent me any longer, and perhaps she never has. Not to mention all the other characters in this collection. I want to call things by their proper names. I believe my writing needs this honesty, this resistance, this courage. I am Vår. Lou is Lou. Not Cyril, as he's called in "Rain Border."

As I'm writing, I'm sitting at my old desk in the homestead in Bø. The drawers are full of archived feelings. One of them is called *Lou and Oscar, Kyoto 2007*. A few days ago, I opened the drawer and reread all the emails they sent me when I was in Japan. And that's when it dawned on me how much more ruthless I am than Ragnhild. You can't trust reality, they say. But I'm willing to take that risk.

This situation between the three of us, has, unhappily, lasted for several years already. Neither Lou nor Oscar was able to pull out of the triangle. They had lost their pride and thus had nothing to lose. I was doubly loved. And I actually think I enjoyed that, in all its simple cruelty. So it ended as it always does: they pushed me into a corner and asked me to choose. My answer was to travel far away, damned if I knew where, to the other side of the world. Where I could wake up in the morning, safe in my knowledge that it was bedtime in Europe. I told them both that I needed to be alone for a while. But the truth is that I needed time to hatch a new plan.

I've changed the last few years, for the worse. I learned to lie to Lou, to deceive; to take risks, while he learned truth and safety from me. Oscar taught me to seek freedom, while I chained him to me with stronger and stronger bonds. Lou once said about me that he'd created a monster. And that made me smile. As if it was a triumph. Because during my childhood, I was kind to a fault.

Thus, I wandered the streets of Kyoto with a new kind of self-confidence: blond, blue-eyed, and chubby-cheeked. I collected stamps from Zen gardens in a little book I'd bought. Now don't misunderstand me: I've never had a particular bond with rocks, with raked gravel or moss. I collected the stamps simply because I liked the idea of filling up the pages of a book. Besides, I had to prove to Lou and Oscar that I spent my time on something useful.

The only garden I really enjoyed was Ryoanji, the temple of the peaceful dragon. The dry landscape was created sometime in the fifteenth century and consists of fifteen rocks, but no matter where you stand, you can only see fourteen at a time. They say that only he who achieves enlightenment can see all fifteen rocks at the same time. I'm telling you this because I believe it's this dead angle I want to write my novel from—that it's there my rottenness is hiding.

I remember Ryoanji so well, not because of the garden itself, but because of what happened afterward. I hadn't checked my email for a long time. I was scared. Scared that Lou and Oscar had talked with each other. I had promised them both that I wouldn't see the other before I left. But I made love to them both in secret, of course.

Apart from Ryoanji, I remember the internet café most of all. It was on the seventh floor, just above a karaoke bar. Computers and colorful one-armed bandits in rows, in a small room that must've been a storeroom previously or something like that. I remember a damp, stuffy atmosphere, closed windows. I was nervous when I opened my inbox, and with reason. It was full of emails from Lou and Oscar. Emails I later printed out, collected in a folder and classified. They are the transcripts I've got on my desk now.

What surprises me when I look through these emails is how similar in yearning they are, as if they were written by the same person. Only word choices vary, different kinds of wordings. But the content is more or less identical. In retrospect I've been thinking about the comedy, or tragedy, of it all: put in the same situation, people usually become the same.

I don't know what you're thinking, but I think it's an exciting topic for a novel. Both Lou and Oscar waited with excitement for me to make the final decision and leave the other. They were trying to give me courage to make my choice by inundating me with their love, both so cocksure. Oscar even sent me a photo I could use to masturbate.

I had to make a choice—that became very clear as I was sitting there shivering, I remember. How long could I continue like that, walking around in Kyoto, alone, without feeing lonely? My book was already filled with stamps from the Zen gardens, I had crisscrossed the city until my heals were covered in blisters, I had taken hot baths with old women in the traditional onsen, I had seen geishas disappearing behind street corners and into cars, I had eaten an abundance of sushi, I'd been a tourist, and now I was longing to go home. But to whom?

I have to admit that I did something pretty banal. I made two lists. One for Lou and one for Oscar. Beneath each name, I wrote what I liked and what I disliked, handed out points. I jotted it down on a used napkin. It's here on my desk right now, with soya-stained edges. When I divided it all up, Lou topped both lists, the positive and negative. I've always wanted to have more rather than less, no matter what it's about, so the choice was clear. I just needed courage to carry it out.

I remember that I logged out of the mailbox and went down to the karaoke bar. I sat there for a while drinking sake and listening to a man in a suit singing French love songs in a strong Japanese accent. The words were indistinct, but the message was impossible to miss. It was as if he directed them to me. As you know, Lou is French. I took it as a sign. Sometimes the world is synchronized. Things just fit. I gulped down the rest of the sake and went up to the café again, opened my mail once more, and started to write to Lou, almost as if in a trance.

My darling Lou, I wrote. *I want you to know that I'm tired of this emotional chaos. I want something simple. Because it's you who are my king. I love you more than ever. Your Vår. PS: I promise to break it off with Oscar*. And I finished with this quote from the monk Thomas Merton: "*One's spiritual life consists of loving. You don't love because you want to do what's good, or to help, or to protect someone. If that's how we act, we see our neighbor as an object and nothing else, and we experience ourselves as generous and wise people. This has nothing to do with love.*" I've no idea where I got this quotation.

The minute I'd sent this letter to Lou, I felt nauseous.

I took a taxi back to the hotel, ran up to my room and threw myself at the toilet. I spent the whole night with my head in the shit, literally. All I could think of was what I'd chosen to lose. I reminisced over my time with Oscar until tears filled my eyes. Thought of things I should've added to his list.

It's strange to sit here in my nursery in Bø and think about this. It's only now, years later, that I feel I have distance enough to touch this material without compassion or sympathy, without this incessant understanding of myself. Without always longing for the poetry of language. Because it didn't stop there. After a few hours hanging over the toilet bowl, I suddenly got an idea. I had a shower, washed away all this repulsiveness, combed my hair, dressed in Lou's dark-brown suit and his light-yellow shirt with horses—the one that used to makeme feel so safe—and jumped into a taxi. I gave the driver the address to the 24-hour internet café.

It was four o'clock in the morning. The karaoke bar was still full of people. This time, a toothless teenager was standing on the stage singing Sex Pistols' "God Save the Queen." If I'd taken a moment to listen for signs this time as well, perhaps I'd stopped there and not continued up the stairs.

There was hardly anyone in the room, but the atmosphere felt even more confined than before, as if there wasn't enough oxygen in there. But as I said, I didn't listen to any signs. Neither did I think. I just found the email I'd sent Lou, copied it, changed the names and sent it to Oscar. I remember that I walked out of the internet café with a feeling of triumph. Then I went straight to a really expensive restaurant and filled my empty stomach with Kobe steak, celebrated my deception. As if I'd done something honorable, liberated myself from all forms of female sentimentalism.

That's what I want to explore in my next novel. This total blindness to oneself, to a situation, to others. The lack of compassion as well, of course. Lack of compassion in writing.

I don't remember so much of the days that followed, apart from walking in and out of shops, buying gifts for Lou, for Oscar, and that I checked my emails several times a day. But my inbox remained strangely empty.

Finally, the emails arrived. Once more it struck me how similar they were. But the tone was totally different. And the font was bigger, and with long breaks between the words. As if they both wanted to make sure that I understood what was written, considering the distance between Europe and Japan. Liar, cheat, hypocrite. Cold, crass, cynical. Lou and Oscar had obviously talked on the phone, I was exposed.

I can really imagine that I could write a whole novel about this, about this lie that unravels like a cheap pair of nylons. Perhaps it's exciting to change perspective as well. Follow Lou walking along the canals in Berlin looking at how the trees are being cut down, one by one. Or Oscar, who locks himself in his room in London, trying to console himself with junk food and porn. But I don't think so. I think I'll stick with my own perspective. The suffering of others has probably never been my field.

Today my skin is beginning to peel. I'm sitting here on the homestead in Bø, in my nursery, tearing off thin layers of dead skin, dead hide. As if I'd been protected by something almost invisible, been wrapped in Glad wrap.

I sat outside in the sun a few days ago, just here at the back of the house. But I didn't manage to stop in time, vanity took over and I became sunburnt. Bright red nose tip. And now my skin is peeling, and I don't think it's accidental. It's the superfluous words that are being deleted from my writing, that's how I see it. I'm thinking that this is where I have to start my next novel. From this fragile place.

My best wishes,
Vår

DUNGENESS

Previously, people didn't notice him, as if he didn't exist. The few who spoke to him soon forgot him, forgot his name and avoided inviting him to parties. He didn't make himself seen or heard either. When he went to his café, he would usually sit in a corner or behind something. Hidden by the sounds of others, he listened to his own thoughts, his pulse, his heart, to the slow beats of life. He pinched his arm without noticing anything. The chairs were soft, so he was often sitting there, slumped. The poor air, the dim lighting, the floral curtains—drawn even in the middle of the day—all this was like a warm duvet he could pull over himself. And when the light outside forced itself in through a crack in the curtains, he took hold of the chair, moved it back and forth, almost like a dancer, to keep his place in the shadows.

But one day the corners are occupied by others. He stands in the doorway, searches the room anxiously, meets a look that dazzles him. By accident, he thinks, because he can't believe that anyone would look at him on purpose. He wants to leave. Stands there, wavering. Hesitates. However, it feels as if the wind is pushing him inside. He sits down at a table in the middle of the large room. Looks inside himself, closes his eyes. For a long time. Until his hair grows long and disheveled and covers them.

With his long, greasy hair he no longer seems quite so anonymous. When he opens his eyes again, many people are sitting at the table with him. He pinches his arm. It hurts. He gets an expression, an impression of being someone. It gives him courage. He pinches his arm again. The bruises create fine patterns on his pale upper arm.

Summer, in a park:

He notices her because she notices him. He observes that she observes him. In backlight. He squints until his eyes are almost hidden behind his eyelids, then he goes and stands in the shadow of a tree. She approaches in an indiscreet, obvious, and insistent way he's unused to, but which he likes. He says his name to her many times, says it and hopes she won't leave without remembering it. She nods in recognition, as if she had heard it before. She comes closer. Now she is in the shadow as well. He can feel her hairs rising on her arms, her breath on his cheek. When he looks at her, it's as if he's blinded by snow, his eyes large and empty as winter.

Then he relaxes, lets go of his look. He thinks she's beautiful, that her charisma borders on melancholy, despite the light of her near-white hair and skin. She looks like an albino. He wants to say something to her, but doesn't know what or how. He's not used to being listened to, but her hesitancy gives him a bit more confidence. She wants to know more about him. Instead, he tries to describe her.

—You're thin in a way that doesn't make you seem skinny, he whispers in her ear. There's something strange in his voice, as if he feels ashamed.

She listens. She doesn't want to miss a word about herself.

—Your cheekbones are very prominent and draw a lopsided line down to your mouth, he continues.

She smiles. She looks as if she's crying when she smiles, he thinks: stunning, staggering, strenuous. He takes her in his arms and holds her tight. They both have thin skin, almost transparent, so their veins show. He doesn't feel comfortable with so much contact so soon. He wants to crush every bone in her body. It's a repulsive thought that feels foreign to him. At once he loosens his grip.

She opens her mouth to say something. He holds his breath.

—How do eyes look that have been blinded by snow?

—White.

—How does a person look who's been blinded by love?

—Lonely.

—How does it feel being blind?

—Black.

—Is it dangerous to look at the sun for too long?

—It hurts your eyes.

—Is it dangerous to lie in the sun for too long?

—It damages your skin so you age more quickly. But for anything else, the sun is a lifegiving blessing that makes things grow.

They look at each other in surprise. He picks up courage and kisses her. She moves inside herself. He follows. She tells him that she's too weak to have her own opinions. That she moves from one relationship to another and stays with whoever desires her the most. At the moment it's him, she says. He nods. She gives him her hand—or is it he who takes hers? They're not quite certain about that. They stand with sweaty palms and hug each other so hard that their blood almost stops circulating. As if not to slip away from each other.

He doesn't quite know where to go, yet it's he who leads the way. He takes her into a narrow and crooked side street. He stumbles a few times, the cobblestones tripping him up. She smiles faintly. With her eyes. And he laughs gently back with his.

Instinctively, without really wanting to, he takes her straight to his favorite café. He stands outside and wonders if they should go inside. A cat runs past them, hisses, disappears into a cul-de-sac. He falters a little; his knees fail him, his courage as well. He lets go of the doorhandle. Doubting, he leads her away, past empty benches, deserted graveyards, along busy roads. Searching, longing for hideouts, alleyways. He wants this trip to last. He almost forgets where they are. She doesn't notice where they're going. She stares at the sun without blinking, as if she had glass eyes.

She asks: What does a person look like after having made love?

—Red, he answers, and pushes her up against a wall, thrusts into her.

When a tomcat fucks a she-cat, his genital cuts her as if with a knife. It is a painful experience that ends in a violent struggle. Like caterwauling in the night that sounds like a baby's cries: desire that has turned sour.

The city:

As soon as she opens the window, the pollution and the noise strike her: cars hooting, breaking, the odd collision. She squints before this artificial scene: neon lights, headlights, lamplights. It's not quite dark outside, even if it's late. She misses the pitch-darkness that can only be found beyond the densely populated areas, where cities cease to be cities. Another form of loneliness, maybe. Outside the window people are crossing the street without looking where they're going, going home with each other without thinking, rushing ahead. That's how she sees him, too: every morning and every evening, coming and going, as if he was a prisoner of time. And in a funny way she does feel imprisoned by him.

She is alone in his flat. It's on the second floor of an old, yellow block. She doesn't listen to music, doesn't read books, doesn't turn on the television.

She closes the window. His flat is full of old-fashioned items. There are candleholders on every table, dresser, windowsill in the living room, with wax stains down to the floor. The walls in the hallway are decorated with sun-bleached photos from unknown people's childhoods. She walks past several times without stopping, glances up cautiously. Then she tears them all down, scrapes off the tape and blue tags and pulls out the drawing pins. Makes a pile of the photographs and shuffles them. Places them on the carpet, one by one. Studies them. A photo of a small boy on a swing catches her attention. Someone has colored in the boy's brown hair and blue shorts, while the background is still black and white. Mud and sea. A flat, endless landscape. She fetches a pair of scissors. Cuts out the boy. Fetches a magnifying glass. Studies the horizontal line. Fails to find a single hill or elevation. At the back of the photo is the name of the place. She takes the atlas down from the bookshelf and looks up D. For Dungeness.

Then she flings herself down in the cracked leather chair with a back looking like a beetle. Her skin sticks to it. She gets goosebumps. Sometimes she thinks that his things are more alive than she is: they give her an uncomfortable impression of being superfluous. Now and then she gets a feeling that the rooms are going to shrink, fold themselves around her and suffocate her. She gets up from the chair, hurries into the kitchen and gulps down a glass of water. On the small shelf above the kitchen sink are two porcelain dolls, naked; but with painted blue eyes, white socks, and black shoes. He found them at the same flea market as the photographs and the atlas, the cracked leather chair, and almost everything in this flat, and he took them all home. It was she who discovered the tiny swastikas afterwards, hidden beneath the synthetic, blond hair. It's as if the dolls are staring into an emptiness, without noticing her, as if she doesn't exist.

This is the same way she sometimes stares through him, past him. Perhaps she's about to forget it: two people who must have felt something for each other, forget how they experienced the first day and all the days after. Perhaps she's about to forget that she knew about him before they met, noticed him before they made eye contact, talked about him before she talked to him. When he said his name, she pretended that she'd never heard it before.

The City:

One day she isn't there. One of his photographs lies on the kitchen table, with a hole in the middle. All that's left is a bleak, flat landscape. And this note from her:

I've gone to Dungeness. Back soon to pick you up.

He walks around the flat. Naked. Confused. Thinking about this word: Dungeness. The photographs in the hallway are mixed up, as if they've been shuffled. He gets a glimpse of himself in the mirror. An old, baroque mirror that distorts his appearance.

He doesn't look as if he's quite awake, with his hair hanging over his face. He turns his eyes inwards until they almost disappear into his skull and only the white is visible. Walks around the flat like a blind man, bumps into things he usually avoids, practicing a pathway.

It's a long time since he has been alone in the flat. He doesn't quite know how to deal with so many feelings without her close by. He collects things he believes will make her smile, wants to make it nice for her. Hangs up a painting of a moose above the bed. Finds a knife, starts to scrape off the candlewax from the floor, from tables and windowsills, too. He plans to wash the windows, clean the bathroom, tidy up the kitchen. But then he suddenly stops in front of her green knee socks, thrown into a corner, and picks them up. He discovers several things, like her dotted skirt on the cracked leather chair. No matter where he walks, he finds signs of her: a bowl of blueberries on the night table, a pair of dirty underpants in the bathroom, bloodied pads in the garbage bin, white hairs in the sink. It's not much, but it makes him happy.

He puts the knife away. Wants the flat to stay the same so that when she comes back, it'll look as if she never left. He walks into the bedroom, takes down the moose painting and puts it in the wardrobe. Opens the fridge and closes it again. His feet are cold. Takes a hot shower but forgets to dry himself. Then he puts on some clothes, a little too tight, too short, but they suit his mood. He's been alone in the flat for long enough now.

The City:

When she returns, she opens all the windows. The exhaust and the city noises don't trouble her so much any longer, she says. The flat's worse. It feels closed in. She complains that there's dust in every nook and cranny. Asks why he didn't do a bit of tidying up while she was away. He tells her of course he could've, but he was so busy with other, more important things. She doesn't ask what, looks out the window instead, absorbed in her own thoughts. It's cloudy, no stars in the sky. Gloomy, as always.

She tries to describe the place where she's been.

—It was beautiful, in a nontraditional, almost unappetizing way, she explains.

He feels that the shadows outside affect her. That she has been stifled just a little, inside. But he doesn't complain. He likes her manner. A bit dark, like the sky in polluted cities. He tries to catch her attention. Places himself in front of the window and asks her to continue.

—The ocean was far away because of the ebbtide, she tells him. I walked in mud for an eternity before I reached the water. I liked how my legs sank into the mud, made me dirty, it seemed silvery in the intrusive light: made my eyes sensitive and aware, made me appreciate things I usually ignore.

She laughs without being aware of it. Continues.

—In the gardens there were stranded boats and the houses were leaning because of the wind. In some of them there were so many holes that you could see straight through the walls, see the flat and endless landscape continuing on the other side. A tiny train sped through the terrain, making lots of sound and pumping thick smoke from its pipe. In the background there was a large and towering nuclear power station.

She tells him that this is the place she'd like to live. That she likes how the surroundings affect her. Mentally. That if he still desires her, he has to follow here there.

He closes the window, pulls the curtains. She's about to say more, but he lays a finger on her lips. They stand like that for a while, in silence. She waits for an answer from him that is not forthcoming. Instead he tears off her clothes. They lie in a pile on the floor. Then he lifts her up, carries her into the bathroom and puts her down on the porcelain sink, yellow-brown around the edges and with white hairs in the drain. He doesn't wait for her to open her legs, just thrusts into her instantly. They loosen now. The words. He whispers some of them in her ear.

The next day they have breakfast together for the first time in a long time. He boils eggs and makes coffee. She sits in the kitchen with a blanket around her, unkempt, white hair. She seems to be looking forward to it already, he thinks, while he's a little worried. Pours coffee into their cups. Then he cuts the top off his egg. It's so hardboiled that it looks almost green. He looks at his watch several times. Places the half-full cup in the sink, puts on his shoes in the hallway and runs out. He must say it. He must say it. He must give notice.

The City:

He hurries home. As he's taking off his shoes in the hallway, he hears a strange male laughing. She's sitting in the living room with someone else. On the table is a half-eaten cheesecake and cups of tea. Lit candles, too. She fetches an extra plate and cuts a piece of cake for him immediately. A few blueberries fall off the top. She picks them off his plate and puts them in her mouth. She tells him that the stranger is an old friend. He notices the tenderness in her voice and in the movements of the stranger. He suddenly thinks that the stranger is more likely an old lover. His hands begin to sweat. He gets up to shake hands. The man's hand is so large and powerful that his almost disappears into it. They exchange names, but he's too nervous to remember it afterwards. The stranger says he likes it here. He's relaxing in the cracked leather chair, lighting one cigarette after another. He says that if everyone agrees, he'd be happy to move in when they move out.

Pause:

They're packing. When she sorts through the things in the wardrobe, she finds the moose painting. She wonders why he hasn't hung it up. She wraps it in silk paper but leaves it there. Then she walks into the living room and gets the antique candleholders, stuffs them into socks and t-shirts and puts them among their things. She asks him to help her with the cracked leather chair. He looks at her as if she's gone mad, but she nods firmly.

But apart from these things, they hardly take anything with them. She says they're not going to be together all that long anyway, that she'll leave him as soon as his desire has been quenched. She decided that a long time ago. He looks at her, astonished. Almost shocked. Because he both loves her and wants her. He has proven that. But he doesn't say anything.

She draws her breath, listens to the sounds outside, cars, to the sounds inside herself, loneliness. Then she closes the windows. Tells him she's looking forward to opening them again, somewhere else. That she can hardly wait. He thinks it sounds good. Fetches the record player and all the vinyl records he has bought at the market. She claims that they don't need music there by the sea, they can listen to the waves instead, to nature's changing songs. He packs them anyway.

She looks into the rooms one last time. Thinks of all the hours, days, months. An unclear picture. Because all the time she's been longing for something else with him. She looks at the pair of dolls on the little kitchen shelf. Puts them in her bag. They leave.

Dislocation:

There are hardly any vacant places on the train. They've squeezed their luggage onto their reserved seats. They remain standing in the aisle. He notices a couple in the carriage through a small crack in the curtain. The man has his hand down the Asian woman's beige Bermuda shorts and moves it violently between her thighs. She leans her head back in pleasure and notices him. Her slanted eyes have no shame, he thinks, as they don't look away. But he turns away: he would rather look into the fair, wide open eyes he knows so well. Together they look out the train window and admire the naked landscape.

They get off the train. She carries the suitcases and the backpack, while he takes care of the cracked leather chair and the record player. Finally, they find the bus stop. He stands waiting on the roadside for a long time, while she sits cross-legged on the leather chair.

When the bus finally comes, they push all their stuff into the luggage compartment beneath. She hurries up to the first floor, almost running. He follows.

To leave the city gives him a strange feeling: He doesn't quite dare to let go. He sits down next to her but turns around all the time. The road is bumpy. She's holding his hand. He notices that hers is cold, not the least sweaty, as usual. He asks if she can tell him again about the place, describe the mud and the nuclear power plant. After a while, he stops looking back, looks forwards instead, until all the bumps in the road rock him to sleep.

Without knowing that his eyes have been closed, he opens them, keen to experience the same things she does. She's still holding his hand. He can feel it tingling. He pulls it out, shakes his bluish fingers. The bus is stationary. The driver is reading an old newspaper, mumbling the program guide out loud to himself and drinking coffee from a child's thermos with faded colors. She's hurrying out, impatient now, and as usual, he follows her.

Autumn, in Dungeness:

The first night in the boathouse, they sleep on the floor, on top of their clothes. He's uncomfortable, tries restlessly to lie on his side, his stomach, his back. His body keeps nudging hers. He can't bear to look at her sleeping with her eyes open, looking at him, without noticing him. He wants to take off his jacket and cover her face. Instead he closes her eyelids as if she were dead.

When he finally falls asleep, he wakes up soon after with her eagerly shaking him. The sun penetrates the room, touches his eyelids, forces him to open them. He is confused, doesn't know where he is. He watches her get up. She has bruises all over her body, her cheeks are red, and his jacket has made funny stripes on her skin. She steps on some dry fish bones with her bare feet, opens all the windows. The sounds of the ocean, of seagulls, of nature he doesn't have words for, overwhelm him. He asks if she has to have the windows open. She's trying to air out the moldy and deserted atmosphere, she explains, taking his hand. She says she wants to make the place theirs, wants the smells the two of them carry to impregnate the walls. He feels worn out and weak. A bit scared, too. But she pulls him up.

They walk out to the mud by the sea that she has told him so much about. It's warm for this time of year. His ears are like snail shells, take in all that's unsaid. And she, with drops of salt water in her hair, is happily reticent.

They move apart, without noticing. Several hours later, they meet again by chance down by the water's edge: two silhouettes in the dark. The only light is from an old lighthouse sweeping across the landscape now and then. They fumble for each other's hands. Finally find them. He tells her he has bought a mattress, duvet, pillows, and bed linen. That it's all waiting for them at home. She smiles so that the slanted line down to her mouth almost curls up. He can't remember having seen her smile like that before. It scares him somewhat, all these new things. She finds a few broken rushes on the ground, picks them up, braids them together and gives it to him. Perhaps they can hang it on the door, she suggests. He holds it firmly so it doesn't blow away. The wind tousles their hair. Her white hair almost covers her whole face. He likes her that way: a bit wild, a bit mad. And he feels dizzy from so much fresh air.

They keep going in the dusk. Away from the sea. Along the road there's a pyramid made of children's shoes. He stops. Looks around, nervous for a moment. The lights are turned off in the few houses they can see along the narrow road.

—It's very quiet here, he says. It's quiet everywhere.

She takes his hand again and pulls him along. Explains that she needs outside peace to feed her internal torment. Asks if he has seen any people today, apart from those in the shop.

He ponders for a minute, then points towards an almost overgrown path.

—At the beginning of that path, two girls were sitting on the ground playing with a rusty rifle. Behind them, a middle-aged man was walking, bent down, looking for worms. The sisters were both beautiful, with red hair, and without a doubt they looked like their ugly father, but his repulsive genes had turned extreme and become attractive.

He keeps thinking, but nothing else comes out.

She pulls him with her towards the sea again. There she takes off her shoes. He does the same. Lets his toes sink down into the mud. The sky is full of stars. She shows him Orion: blinded as a punishment for love. Who got his sight back by staring at the sun through the whites of his eyes. He asks if they should go home to bed.

The mattress is put in the middle of the room. The bed linen is black, like a hole you're dragged down into, he thinks, and likes that it is a bit unpleasant, almost creepy. She, on the other hand, says that this blackness, this darkness, lights up her skin, her thoughts. She says she loves the feeling of lying down on new bed linen, on a new mattress, under a new duvet. Like the evening before, she falls asleep almost at once, while he lies awake. He looks at the white back of her head. She turns and hits him without meaning to. He hits her back, without her noticing it. Finally, he relaxes, lets go. Falls asleep. He dreams that her old friend calls from the city flat, asking if they've had sex yet in the boathouse. He crawls closer to her. Imagines that he's making love to her in all sorts of ways, that she rides on him until he gets a cramp. But she doesn't touch him. Her body, bloody and moody, doesn't have the patience to be with him tonight. He kisses her instead, the taste of menstruation on his tongue, masturbates. She doesn't wake up. Sleeps like a log throughout this night, and many nights ahead. Heavily.

It takes him some time to get used to her, here. For a long time he wakes up without a sense of place, the city still in his guts.

Still, slowly, he settles down, finds his roots. The sounds through the window in the morning, in the evening, the bird-songs, wind, rain, the sounds of the ocean, of weather, and once in a while, people, steps, and even more rarely, conversations, words. He's learnt to like all this.

Dungeness:

She has forgotten why they're there.

—Why isn't important, he says, as long as you're with someone like me.

He feels that this is the most important role of his life.

She eats blueberries that color her teeth, lips and hands. She reminds him of a small child, or something that's fading away. He doesn't know which. He still enjoys watching her lick her fingers, sucking them one by one, with her blueberry tongue.

She tells him her teeth grew in her first, then the legs, before hair, and that last were her breasts. But never at the same time. He studies her eyes while she's talking. Only now does he discover that her eyelashes continue all the way around, even in the small corners reserved for tears. They remind him of the work of a spider, or even the spider itself. He is afraid that if he looks at them for too long, he'll be caught and eaten like an insect. A fly, maybe. So he never looks for too long, just in secret, when she forgets that he's there.

He remembers that his body hurt during puberty. His sex ached for almost a year. His shoulders, legs, upper body. But the pain was strongest where his consciousness was. Where it still is.

Dungeness:

A car is coming. It reminds her of the city, of people who are creeps. The car's a small dot she follows with her eyes until it becomes big and recognizable.

Yellow car. Beetle.

Often, when she has a new man, her mother comes for a visit. That's just how it is. She's almost a little hurt that her mother hasn't come before. She can feel it now, that she's been waiting for this meeting. She asks him to give her a nice reception, doesn't explain why she's leaving, puts on her rubber boots and goes out the back way, out into the mud.

Her mother runs out of the car. She seems happy to see him, although she doesn't know him. He looks at this unfamiliar woman with familiar features. She has grey-white hair pulled firmly back and wrinkles in the corners of her mouth and around the eyes. He looks at these eyes. They are fair, almost transparent, like those of a blind person. And with eyelashes all the way around, just like her daughter's eyes. He tries to look somewhere else, to tear himself away, but can't stop staring.

Her mother doesn't seem surprised that her daughter isn't there. It surprises him. He tells her his name. Many times. Her mother laughs. She promises not to forget it. He shows her around. There isn't much to show: the few things he insisted on bringing, like the vinyl records, which he doesn't listen to anymore, just like she'd predicted. Most of their things are still in the city flat. He didn't understand it then, that the foaming ocean, the insects, yes, even some of the smells, were things that would set the tone of their life together. And in a strange way, he likes this material emptiness, the feeling of having just moved in. He likes it because it was her choice. Because she is so beautiful when she gets her own way.

He explains, explains away, mostly to himself. The boathouse is cool. They sit down in the front. The sun is shining unabashedly. Her mother looks at it. He notices that her armpits are sweaty. There are two dark spots on the synthetic material of the sweater. He doesn't know what to say, so instead he keeps talking.

—In the course of one day, you can experience many different lights, many colors, he says.

He maintains that it's because the place is so flat. The sky covers it like a lid. Beneath the lid, behind windows, behind masks, live the Dungeness people. Many of them look a little too much like each other.

He shows her mother a garden of destroyed tools, fishing gear, shells, snail shells, rocks, driftwood, local plants, bushes, and anything you can pick up from a junkyard. He can see that her mother isn't listening. That her thoughts are somewhere else. With her daughter, perhaps. He wonders where she is—until he sees her out in the ocean. She's wading farther and farther out.

Suicide: the best way to take your own life is to cut along the artery with something sharp, then lie down in a bathtub filled with hot water, wait for the blood, for thoughts and time, to flow out, for your body to fill with something other than fear.

He goes inside. He doesn't feel like saying anything else today. His throat is dry. Her mother follows him. He makes coffee for her even though she says she prefers tea.

She looks at him for a long time.

—You're caught, aren't you? she says.

He looks down, takes a big swig of the coffee, burns his tongue, keeps his words inside, swallows. Her mother swigs her coffee and calmly holds out the cup. He has to keep filling it up. She has a lot of things to say that he doesn't want to hear. He wants to tell her to stop, but instead he asks her to continue. He stands by the window. Sees her daughter in the ocean, still there. She's going to get sick, he thinks, he hopes, and takes another sip of coffee. He can't follow what her mother's saying. Like when there's a bad phone connection, his responses keep falling a little behind. It doesn't seem to matter to her. Instead, she takes out a pack of cards from her bag and puts them in front of her on the floor. From the corner of his eye he sees her draw a card, then another. Her hands are shaking. The place gets dark. He closes his eyes.

Finally, her mother leaves. Without saying hello to her daughter. And when she comes back from the sea, she doesn't ask about her mother.

Dungeness:

She sits in the cracked leather chair in front of the window. He thinks at first that she's asleep. But her eyes are so strange, almost frighteningly wide open, and her mouth is moving, making sounds, saying words. He feels her forehead. She is sweating, has a fever. He likes how it affects her. The dullness of her eyes.

—I saw a dog the other day, she whispers, about a week ago. A lovely dog with grey, almost green fur. But when I saw his prick, I discovered that he didn't have balls. Just a few stitches after an operation.

He looks at her while she speaks, her eyes blank, red. He wants to put a needle into them to leak out all the fluid.

—Continue, he says.

—The dog, Takashi was his name, caressed the stitches, licked them. He seemed happy. The dog's owner told me that he castrated him to give him a longer life. He looked as if he loved him, and the dog seemed happy enough, so I suppose there was nothing wrong with what he'd done. The owner said that when Takashi reached puberty, he became so possessed by licking bitches that he didn't want to play anymore. That when he discovered his sexuality, he became boring. The owner thought the castration would grant the dog a new life, new pleasures that didn't have to do with sex. He told me that he too liked licking pussy, that he had been jealous of Takashi now and then, his lack of inhibition.

—Continue, he repeats.

She closes her eyes better to remember.

—We walked together to the owner's house. An old, windswept boatshed. The half-rotten wooden beams were painted copper-red, but the paint was beginning to chip, like sunburnt skin peeling. Inside, on a chair in the hallway, a woman sat reading a book. He nodded to her, and then went into the kitchen to make tea. I followed. While he made the tea and chatted with the dog, he suddenly pulled me to him and started kissing me like mad. Then he asked me to go into the living room, take off my panties, lie down on the table and spread my legs. He said he'd come to me in a couple minutes.

She stops, uncertain whether she should continue.

—Continue, he insists, without looking at her.

—I did as he asked, she admits. Obeyed him, like a dog obeys his owner. I took off my panties, lay down on the cold living room table, on top of the white tablecloth, a bit dirty, my bum bare. I was surrounded by breadcrumbs and a half-empty wine bottle. I waited. Heard him talking to the woman. He asked her if she liked the book. She said no, but she'd continue to read it anyway, as they didn't have any other books in the house. Then he came over to me, placed his head between my thighs and started to lick me.

She stops abruptly.

—Continue!

—At a certain point, the phone rang. The dog owner answered it, opened his fly and spoke to someone briefly while I sucked him off. Then we went back to the kitchen and drank Japanese smoked tea with the reading woman.

After this, she doesn't speak for a while. She has already said more than she thinks he can take.

The days pass, but he can't get the story out of his head. One night, when he's lying close to her, he asks her to tell it to him again. Asks her to help him get a clearer picture. He wants to focus on the table, where she was lying, what she sensed. She pretends to be asleep, but in the morning, she decides to talk. He puts his hand down his briefs as she tells him what she saw from the living room table: the big windows with a view to the nuclear power plant, the stranded boats, everything he has become fond of. She tells him that Takashi, the dog, was watching them all the time. She thinks that he's now living his sexuality through his owner, who had the loveliest prick she'd ever seen, almost purple. When she left, he promised to think about her for a while.

—For many days, she admits, I could feel the tickling from his tongue.

That's all she says, waiting for a reaction from him.

Almost nothing comes.

He takes his hand from his briefs, clears his throat, and drinks a glass of water. It sticks to his throat. Tastes bitter.

—To think of something beautiful makes me sad, he then says, almost apologetically, and tries to kiss her, but his tongue feels sedated.

He continues to tell her it isn't how she thinks it is. The way she predicted. That despite what she probably imagines, he desires her still.

Pause:

He looks at her from the side and thinks that there's something he really likes about her, he's sure of that, but he can't remember what it is. Now it seems that he might have lost it. He has seen a man looking at her, smiling. He thinks again that he has lost it, that someone else has found it. Only when that other person loses it can she be his again.

Winter:

They almost don't touch each other. The cold has laid itself like a wall between them. It's foggy outside. There are glimpses of fishing boats in the distance. The wind's howling. Inside she invents small, erotic stories to try to satisfy him. His hand that moves in an even and recognizable rhythm behind his fly both irritates and saddens her. She can feel his breath on her neck while she talks. She knows that he no longer has any shame. That he can imagine anything. She notices that he is anxious, tense. That he likes what she tells him in a way that hurts. He tries to smile, but his lips are sore, especially in the corners of the mouth. He gets the Vaseline and rubs his lips, then his whole face. Ever since he was a small boy, he has used Vaseline to keep his skin soft. He covers his skin with a thick layer every night before bed. When he's crying, he rubs Vaseline beneath his eyes. That must be the reason he doesn't have any wrinkles, she often thinks. She thinks that's ugly, almost frighteningly so. She wants to see marks from the happiness and the pain that life has inflicted on him. But his face is empty.

—I'm in that middle phase, he explains, where I should've been happy, but I'm actually depressed. I can't quite explain why I'm making myself feeling so nauseous.

He asks if she has met the man with the dog again.

—No, she says.

But she admits that she has called a previous lover and told him about the incident. He became aroused and asked her to ring him more often. When her desire for the dog-owner becomes unbearable, she does.

He asks if she can tell him, too, yet again. She doesn't want to.

—To think about something sad makes me happy, he says then. I know it's hard to understand, but that's how I am.

Dungeness:

Far from the city, she no longer remembers how they met and why. She's often out, in other places. She says she's going to the movies, but there isn't a movie theater in Dungeness. She travels a long distance on the tiny train to watch the big screen. She says the darkness makes her feel comfortable. He never asks her what she has seen. Instead, he tries to get her attention, asking her if she likes his long hair. She doesn't.

He grabs the scissors and goes down to the sea. It's cold and bleak outside, not the least bit beautiful. It's raining, it's sleeting, it'll soon be hailing too. The wind is whistling softly. It sounds like a foreign language he can't understand. All the houses and the boatsheds are in darkness, except for theirs. He closes his eyes, doesn't want to know what he's going to look like. His hair falls into the sea in large tufts. His hands are frozen. He's inaccurate, careless.

He goes into the boatshed again. Almost runs. Finds her sitting in the cracked leather chair, her face turned towards the window. He whispers her name several times, but she does doesn't turn around. He walks closer, stands in front of the window so she can look at him with her wide-open eyes that he loves too much. But she's asleep. He closes her eyes, gets a good hold of her body, heavy from sleep, and carries her to bed. He removes her clothes. His own too. Then he lies down beside her.

When she wakes up the next morning, she looks at him, looks at his close-cropped hair and begins to miss the long mane.

Oblivion is a gradual process in which memory is mislaid.

She forgets him while he's looking at her, a little more every day. He tries to tidy her thoughts. He irons. Everything. Folds her panties, stacks the newspapers alphabetically, the music according to the number of instruments, feelings according to dates. But instead of making things clearer, he almost disappears, as he sits there in the cracked leather chair, his back erect, his legs straight, his body washed, his hair short, his skin clean. Forgotten.

Dungeness:

He takes her hand, holds her hard, forces her to touch him: his nose, his cheekbones, his nipples, his prick.

She opens the door and goes out. He follows. A feeling of heaviness fills him, as if he's standing under water, his pockets filled with rocks. He doesn't hear what she's saying, because she's not saying anything. He pulls her white hair in desperation. She doesn't resist. Not even when he pushes her head down into the almost congealed mud does she struggle. He looks at her dirty face, scratched, unappetizing. He sees that there are remains of mud on her lips. Sees a small insect crawling down into her sweater.

The winter is cold. The frost penetrates the bones, down to the brain. The tip of his nose is red, his earlobes too. When he opens his mouth, frost-breath comes out, but no sound. He wants to apologize to her, but he can't. Thinks: Hurtful things only happen when you're trying to hide them. He slides his fingers under her clothes, down her warm bum crack. Pushes them so far in that she closes her eyes. He pulls them out, smells them, stuffs them into her mouth. He still doesn't get a reaction, an erection, and it makes him lose heart. He tears off her skirt, pantyhose, and underwear. Lets his own trousers fall down to his knees, but can't get it up. He lets her go, full of shame. She picks up her clothes from the ground and disappears into the boathouse. He pulls up his trousers. Stands motionless while she's running from one window to another.

After a while she comes running out again, fully dressed, wearing a beanie, warm jacket, a grey backpack on her back. He wants to say something to her, but the only sound comes from the birds in the sky, the waves in the sea. She runs along the shore, until he can't see her any longer. The lighthouse lights up the road, but she's gone.

The shame chases him into the boathouse. He observes the

terrible mess she's made. One doll has disappeared. The wardrobe doors are wide open and clothes are strewn across the floor. He picks them up patiently, folds them, and puts them back into the wardrobe. He wants it to look nice and tidy when she comes back. A cutting of a small boy falls from the back pocket of one of her pants. He puts it in his breast pocket. He goes into the bathroom, removes the dirty toothbrush glass, exchanges it for a clean one, and puts two new toothbrushes in. He wonders what else he can do to make her happy. He opens the fridge, takes out fish, butter, cheese, and milk. Then he gets flour, salt, and pepper from the cupboard. He begins to clean the fish. While it's boiling, he crumbles the butter into the flour. He follows an old English recipe. When he has finished the preparations, he puts the fish pie in the oven, on very low heat. Waits. Sets the table for two. Opens a wine bottle. Fills the glasses. Gulps his down, then hers.

He removes the fish pie from the oven and eats his part. Puts the rest in the fridge for her. After a while the wine bottle is empty. Outside it gets darker and darker. He looks at the stars, searches for Orion, can't find it. He becomes filled with anxiety but tries not to give in to it.

When he finally goes to bed, he leaves all the lights on so she can find her way back. He lies pressed into his side of the mattress all night long. But her side remains empty, cold.

A flat, desolate landscape:

The next day he gets up at the crack of dawn. He looks at the thermometer: his whole body reacts to the temperature. Wonders where she could've taken cover in this cold weather. He runs panic-stricken in the direction of where he last saw her: along the shore, towards the nuclear plant. He looks at all the boathouses.

Then he suddenly stops. Pauses in front of one that looks like all the others yet still stands out. It's newly renovated, freshly painted. A ladder and bucket of paint stand along one wall. He wants to move towards the window but is scared of what he's going to see: her lying on the table, perhaps, in her green knee socks, her dotted skirt. He imagines her spread legs, her pink labia and white pubic bush. Suddenly he finds himself fantasizing that a big hairy spider is coming out of her cunt. He pictures how it crawls out from her labia, down onto the table, across the tablecloth, down the table legs, all the way to the floor. Then the dog owner steps on it without noticing, because he has his head between her thighs.

He puts his cold fingers down his trousers, until he can't feel his body anymore, his thoughts. He sees his image reflected in the window. He walks to the entrance, puts his hand on the door. It's locked. Not a sound to be heard.

He walks home, his head bent. When he approaches the boathouse, he glances quickly up and notices that all the lights are on inside. He runs over, tears open the door, shouts enthusiastically. But everything is exactly as he left it.

He turns off the light, sits down in the cracked leather chair, and looks out the window with empty eyes. Only now does he begin to realize that she may not be coming back. He's suddenly overcome by a terrible anger. Gets the rest of her things. Packs them in a suitcase.

Then he gets the telephone and calls her mother. He asks her what he should do. She doesn't say much, except that she did warn him, told him this would happen. Then she gives him a few phone numbers. Tells him that her daughter may be with one of these men. He thanks her, puts the phone down. Picks it up again immediately, starts to dial. Different male voices answer. Nobody knows who he is, where she is. Finally he hears a voice he recognizes. He asks her old friend if she's there, almost screams at him. Imagines his big, powerful hands on her fragile body.

He hangs up before her friend can answer.

He walks out onto the doorstep with her suitcase. Just stands there for a while, staring, without knowing what to do or where to go.

Solstice is when the moon moves in front of the sun and everything goes silent. No dogs barking, birds singing, trees rustling, water rippling. Silence.

—We all look the same in the dark, he mumbles while he clutches the handle of the suitcase.

He hopes that she is close by and can hear it.

He waits for a while. A while longer. Before he goes inside. Puts her suitcase in the cupboard in the hall, walks into the bedroom, pulls the mattress into a corner, lies down, and pulls the duvet up over his ears. When he was a small boy, he could lie like that for days. As if he didn't exist.

Invisibility depends on the eye of the beholder. A thing or a person can seem invisible without really being it. But if you follow the laws of physics, invisibility is defined as something that doesn't reflect or absorb light. Thus, by definition, an invisible person must be blind.

Pause:

When he finally pulls the duvet from his eyes, he no longer knows what day it is. His back hurts, he's hungry and thirsty.

He covers himself with the clammy duvet, shuffles into the kitchen, opens the fridge, and drinks a glass of milk gone sour. He takes out the bread and makes himself a banana sandwich. Dry and brown. He eats, standing, looking out on the flat winter landscape: faded, as if there were hardly any colors at this time of year.

He saunters along the shore, looks up at the houses and boathouses. Many of them are empty at this time of year. They say most people only come to Dungeness in summer. But even then there aren't all that many people here.

Back home again, he goes into the kitchen, gets the moldy fish pie from the fridge and throws it in the bin. He moves the mattress from the corner of the bedroom back to the middle. As he does, he sees a spider web: the dust has got stuck to the gluey silk threads that hang down like streamers. He is about to wipe it away but decides to leave it. When the sun shines on it, it looks like a snow crystal.

He doesn't know what to do with his life, so he decides to become interested in other people's lives. He sneaks around in the empty summer houses. He usually finds the keys under the doormat or in a flowerpot. He loves feeling like a stranger: breaking into other people's intimacy. The first thing he does is to remove the sheets from tables and chairs and air out the deserted and dust-filled atmosphere. That's how he makes himself at home: looking at their photos, reading their diaries and letters, writing small greetings in their visitor's books, walking around in strange people's slippers.

Once, he sleeps in a strange bed. He lies there all night with a pounding heart.

He becomes more and more brave. Soon he doesn't worry whether the houses are empty or not. He's like he used to be. Someone hiding in the corners. Someone nobody notices. It's in the way he holds his body, the way he lowers his eyes, that he can get away with these things.

The loneliness of Dungeness didn't used to worry him so much. But now that it's no longer something he can share with her, it feels unbearable. But he still doesn't go back to the city; he fears the loneliness among other people even more.

He walks slowly into the sea, collects small round pebbles and puts them in his pockets. He gets wet; the water seeping into his boots, his cold toes. He becomes numb, turns towards the boathouse. Empty. Just a stray dog runs past.

The pebbles are rubbing holes in his pockets. He takes one out and studies it: grey, with a hole in the middle you can see through. He puts his eye close to it. Feels how smooth it is. Clenches it so hard that his hand almost stiffens.

He walks and walks. Until he arrives at the newly renovated boatshed on the shore. Then he stops. A flock of birds flies over the house. He looks at the patterns they make. He wishes he could tell her how beautiful he thinks it is. He looks at the boats, too, glued into the frozen ground.

He's still holding the pebble. He relaxes his hold and throws it at the largest window. There's just a hollow sound, then the pebble falls to the ground. He waits. It's cool outside, but comfortably so. The spring's here soon, he thinks, and feels a dread: flowers coming up from the earth, leaves growing on trees, becoming green, birds of passage returning, all the things that are good. He thinks: That makes people come here as well. He walks closer to the boathouse. Tries to see through the windows, but the sun dazzles him. He tries the door. It's still locked. He looks under the doormat, in all the flowerpots, but still no key.

Finally he returns to his own place. Empties his pockets and puts the pebbles next to the porcelain doll. It stares up at him. These doll-eyes that won't let him go, make him feel unwell. As if they want to blame him for one doll being separated from the other.

He finds the record player and blows the dust off the needle. Rummages through his old vinyl records. Sinks down in the cracked leather chair while classic music plays softly in the background. He waits for his badly cut hair to grow out again. Looks down at his balls.

Dungeness:

After she disappeared, her mother started visiting. He likes to sit at the window, waiting for the yellow Beetle to appear. Get the coffee or tea ready. Cut the cheesecake, the one he made from her recipe that has a thick layer of blueberries on top. Comb his short hair.

He likes to study her mother. Her skin is full of wrinkles, as if it had been cut with a knife. He looks for marks in the wrinkles that her daughter might have inflicted.

She looks at him, smiles faintly, longingly.

—You too are beginning to look like her, she says.

He looks away. She pulls him with her into the bathroom. She shows him in the mirror that his eyelashes continue all the way around as well, even in the small corners reserved for tears. Besides, his cheekbones seem to be more prominent than before, and a lopsided line running down to his mouth.

He's thinking that her mother visits so often now because he's the closest she can come to her daughter. Because her mother hasn't heard from her either. They're united in this longing. This anger. This deprivation, this yearning, maybe.

Spring:

One day her mother opens her suitcase and dresses in her daughter's clothes: the green knee socks, the dotted skirt. He stands passively watching as she walks out the door, down to the sea in her stockinged feet.

He himself goes into the bedroom and looks at the spiderweb. This is something he often does when a fly has got caught in it. He studies it: how the small, transparent wings beat, how it fights. The silken threads are dusty and have almost lost their stickiness. After a while it manages to free itself and fly away.

He looks out the window at her mother. She's walking along the shore in the green knee stockings. From a distance, there's hardly any difference between mother and daughter. He notices a wrench inside. The sense of loss. That he becomes hard. Stiff. Between his legs. That he can easily be fooled. He decides to follow her.

He pulls down his zipper and lets his pants fall down to his knees. Her mother comes closer. She looks at him, asks him to pull his pants up, asks if there's something she can do. He shakes his head, thinks sadly that she looks old.

Her mother walks up towards the boathouse. Picks up a hoe and putters around in the garden. He follows along, like a dog, sits down on the stoop and gives her some of the round pebbles with a hole in the middle. She uses them as decorations.

After a while she sits down in front of the entrance with him. They look out on the flat landscape, unending and ominous, like a memory. They look out on the sea. Empty without her. The sound of wind, of weather, of fishermen. They look at the nuclear plant, at the lighthouse, at everything she loved.

—You were only supposed to be together for a short while, her mother says. You loved her because you were going to lose her. I'm sure of that.

ALONE IS NOT THE SAME AS LONELY

For want of someone to talk to, I flee into my memories, to another me, immature, unfinished.

It's summer and I've seen more of my mother than I want to. The smell of summer is very close to the smell of sex. It's warm, moist, sweet-and-sour. Almost like chop suey. My genitals smell of summer. The summer when I was fifteen. That's when I discovered myself. At that time, I smelled more of summer than sex. Now I smell more of sex than summer.

This is how I remember it:

My mother strutting naked around the house in a very provocative manner: She reads naked, eats naked, and ignores me naked. I look at her almost all the time. Impossible not to. I search for something to like or to hate, a detail I can concentrate on. I can't find anything other than her yellow shoes. But I'm really smitten with them. I want them, want to take them from my mother, tear them off her. She doesn't deserve to have something so beautiful. I look at my mother again. She shaves her armpits just to satisfy my father. I think: Everything about my mother is so beautiful that it borders on being ugly. Her whole character exists in that, in this borderland.

—You have a rare erotic aura, my mother says suddenly. I'm sure you masturbate a lot. I want you to stop.

—I've just started, I answer.

Mother is without conventions. Without a mother's role. Indecent.

The heat is penetrating. It's supposed to be the hottest period of the year. Drops of water trickle out from every pore of our bodies, as if we're raining.

—Your father's a very good lover, she says then, provoking.

—I know, I answer, surprised.

Father stands up abruptly and smacks me hard on the chin, so it turns read and swollen, but I'm not the least ashamed. I smile. My skin is heated, sore, almost like a vagina. I feel horny and turn the other cheek.

—I'm sorry, he says. I didn't mean to hurt you.

—I know, but I liked it, I answer.

My father hits me again and begins to cry. I try to comfort him, comfort his eyes. I feel like a mature woman in a child's body.

That night I see Mother and Father making love for the fourth time. Mother's on her knees in front of Father and can't get enough. The copulation attracts insects. Mother's cheeks are red and full of flies. I enviously peep at her, because I too want Father. Her veins look as if they're close to bursting. I see images of a growing tree beneath her skin. I find two see-through panties and a bra in the bathroom. Several pairs of stilettos line the hallway. I walk into Father's office and masturbate.

—You have a rare erotic aura, I tell myself loudly. I'm sure you masturbate a lot. Never stop doing that. Because that's the only sure thing. The only thing you can always do.

It's fifteen years since I was fifteen years old. I pull my fingers out of my vagina, smell them, smell me, my desire, my loneliness. I look at myself in the mirror. I see Father in the mirror image, deformed, in me, like a child. I can see that he's crying. I think about words such as blood, incest. The fact that I'm not ashamed makes me feel embarrassed.

Masturbation is a form of reconciliation with the memory. I don't feel alone anymore—but with Father, somewhere in the past.

I don't know why I am: escaping from reality, detached from reality, only that I prefer the memory. The freedom to misremember. To edit. Just that I'm attracted to what I'm repelled by. To do what's wrong, what's shameful. Little things like eating cherries with Father and using my tongue to make knots on the stems.

This is how I remember it:

The juice is red and flows down between our legs. I tell Father that he's the only one who makes me feel like a woman. He's crying again. He can't take it. What's happening between us. That I don't stop it.

He says:

—When I suffer from this, I want to vomit. I try to feel, try to control the feeling of being horny. The only way to control it is to avoid it, and the only way to avoid it is to shut yourself out from it.

—Shh, I whisper, shh.

I dry his tears. Then I lie down on the sofa. Pull Father towards me.

I want him to tell me about Mother: again and again, until I become sore.

He's weak. We are united in this weakness. He explains it like this: that I'm Mother and him, melted together.

I ask him what arouses Mother, sexually.

He says:

—The inside of thighs and the line down to the bum.

He also says:

—Mother often pretends to be asleep. I like that we both lie. I let her believe that she's tricked me. And Mother knows she hasn't tricked me. I think she lets me suffer because her beauty demands it. And that I'm willing to do anything. For her beauty. I want to bite her in her newly shaved armpits. Try something new. I lie down next to her. I can feel the muscles of her vagina moving. Moving around something. Her lips are stiff and dry, but open while I'm growing. I push through her stomach, beneath her skin and take Mother in her sleep. I want her to wake up with a penis between her legs, twisting her body back and forth, moving her mouth in a new way, screaming, being sexual.

I grasp Father's balls hard and squeeze.

—Sorry, I say and squeeze harder.

Father looks at me in pain.

—I don't like you to talk about Mother, I say.

There are only a few incidents in my life that don't concern Mother and Father. I'm alone in the quietness they've left behind. More or less. I live at the top of a block of flats with a view across the whole city. It's dark. The city's twinkling. I want to throw myself out. Float. It frightens me how the force of gravity pulls and tears at me. My longing.

Somewhere out there between the cars, flats, and noises, I imagine him between the legs of any woman. Weak. It hurts. The thought of Father perhaps sleeping with someone else than me.

He may be described in a few words I can't choose between. He is: remnants of a beautiful man who's letting himself go. Perhaps that's what attracted me then, the dilapidation. The memory of how he looked long before I was born.

To remember is just a narcissistic action. I agree with that. But I've nothing against narcissism. I keep remembering things I ought to have forgotten. I'm thinking about when we made love. The first time we made love. That Father was the first I'd ever made love to. That he had pulled me in all sorts of directions. As if arms and legs were separated from the body. That's how it was. Almost. Because nothing's ever the way it really was.

Father says we mustn't concern ourselves with it, his misfortune. All he wants is for me to love him. Always. Even if he can't love me back. Never.

—That, he says, is a true proof of love. Unconditional.

—That, I say, is suicide.

When I get angry, I say:

—I hope that one day I can forget you for someone else. A man totally different from you. A man, more like a boy. My own age.

When Father gets angry, he says:

—Without me, you're nothing, not even beautiful. Because no one can appreciate you the way I do. No one can see what I see.

Then we turn out the lights. I let him get used to the darkness, so it's easier to get used to me. All I see is the light pink of his nipples. I can't even hear his breath, but I can feel my own unbearable smell.

This is how it was:

I stroke Father while he licks me.

—You taste of tar, he asserts. This indescribable color that's more like a smell. This black-brown, viscous liquid that reminds me of summer. It almost feels like licking velvet. It's glistening in the same way and is even softer to the touch.

My ears are burning and my body's shaking.

—Big ears on small girls, I like that, Father says.

He's already found my clitoris. I can feel that I'm soon climaxing. I bend my body upward, and it transforms into a living fountain watering Mother's orchids. I scream. Father nods but doesn't come. My nails have marked his penis.

Father says that his pleasure is to last. To deny himself climaxing. He continues to talk. For a while. He says it's difficult to satisfy him, but that he usually satisfies. He says the only one who satisfies him is Mother.

He repeats:

—Mother.

I think: Every time I watch Father and Mother making love, Mother looks a little younger, she suddenly looks like a little girl.

I lie in the fetal position as if I'm asleep.

Father whispers:

—Mother knows nothing. Mother must never know anything.

Then he puts his fingers in my hole again.

I say:

—Father, I have to pee.

—Pee, he says.

And that's what I do.

Father thinks it's disgusting at first, but it doesn't smell too much and almost tastes like water. Sweet, sugary water.

The memory stops there, in the darkness. I just remembered a certain loneliness. I've looked up all the words in a dictionary and found that they fit. Denial. Constipation. Suppression.

I look at the clock that's ticking. Slowly. And this evening that never ends.

I stand longingly by the window.

The only living thing in my flat is what's happening there. Far away. On the other side of the city. It's blowing outside, the sky's the kind of sky, the moon the kind of moon, that hints of the coming of snow. I don't like snow in big cities. Wet snow with anonymous footprints. Dirty snow. I'm already looking forward to it melting, this snow that's not yet here.

I pull the curtains, shut out the world. Then I sit in the armchair with Mother's yellow shoes on my feet. I don't have a single picture on the walls, not of Mother or Father. My flat is a place without new marks, new feelings. Incidental.

I pull a thick jumper over my nightgown. They say this is the coldest time of year. My breath is mist; I feel the frost inside.

I spit on my fingers and let them slide into my anus. I suddenly remember what Father said about Mother: she was sure the male G-spot was there, under all the shit. I look at my nails: long, well-groomed, with black fingernails and a strong smell.

RAIN BORDER

The first thing he does when she wakes up is to tell her how much he loves her. He says he wants a child: a little girl with light in her eyes. Totally opposite to her, but still her, still them. That's his greatest wish. He kisses her body all over. Asks how much she loves him.

Her hands are clammy. Fighting against the lump in her throat. Her mute voice cracking, the unspoken words. Every morning: I love you. Every night: I love you. Several times a day: I love you.

—I don't know, she whispers.

He looks at her as if she's speaking a foreign language.

—I don't know, she repeats.

Ragnhild wakes up with a start, sits up on the futon and looks around. It takes a little time before she recognizes her things. Next to her, a hairbrush covers a plate with a half-eaten sandwich. On the walls there are lumps of blue tack, but still no cards, no posters. The books are thrown carelessly across the desk. And in the middle of the room there are two piles of clothes: one dirty, one clean. She lacks everything, has everything. A whole world in just one room. Still, she relaxes at the sight of this mess, the freedom of it. Slowly, almost without noticing it herself, she slumps down on the futon again. Listens to Tizane practicing the accordion in the next room, and her cat Aurora sharpening her claws against the thin wall that divides their rooms. She tries not to be disturbed by the weather forecast from the flat above, but it's a crackling sound, as if someone has caught a radio signal from far away. She catches the odd word, such as "Regen," "Schlack," and "Schnee."

As a child, Ragnhild always loved snow: on television, the small dots when the program had finished. Or the chaotic atmosphere in the schoolyard when it became covered in white. How the big boys in elementary school threw snowballs at her. Their clumsy fists, snatching hitting. The snow melting, running down her back, her little bum, and that made her sick for days afterwards. But she was most preoccupied with the boy who put pebbles inside the snowballs. The thin one. With the freckles. At home she made drawings of him with a yellow felt-tip pen. Put them under her pillow. Cyril knows that too. She has told him almost everything, before.

But not this: How it is to wake up, without him. With a start. Not to have his warm, thin, scrawny body to nuzzle against. Not to have his breath in her face. Or his fresh smell that reminds her of wet earth. Not to fight over the duvet: cold feet, cold shoulders, cold bum. To wake up and lie crosswise in the big new coconut-smelling futon instead. Or wake up on the floor, for no reason, in the dust. The quietness to think, to remember a dream. This emptiness, this joy, this hopelessness that loneliness is, which she has never told him about. Or how she is cold on her own, this morning.

She pulls the duvet up to her ears. Without his arms to drag her up, she can lie like this in the futon for hours on end. She looks over at the old coal stove in the corner of the room. She has been warned against the winter in Berlin. Everything gets very cold, they say. She'll get cold. He'll get cold. Faces blue with frost, grey sky. But then she looks out on the half-naked tree outside the window and thinks that that, too, will become beautiful.

She picks up courage, gets out of bed, wraps the blanket around her and walks over to the curtainless windows. The branches of the tree scrape faintly against the pane, the leaves come off, fall to the ground. Some stick to the glass. Her eyes glide farther out, in the direction of Cyril's place. They fall on a river of train rails. Like an umbilical cord they tie her to the core of the city, to him. Behind the rails she glimpses Mauer Park that lights up the night so beautifully when the football stadium is lit. Now and then she goes there, sits on one of the big swings.

She likes to live up on the hill. Where you get the whole view. It feels freer, as if there is more air. But today she'll go all the way down into the valley, where the sun is still shining, perhaps. Where it's often greener, better, but where the air also feels heavier, muggier.

She imagines his flat on the other side of town, tidy now, emptied of her things, emptied of all the things that are here, around her. On the floor. She thinks about the time before she left. The last days when they slept in different rooms, in different beds. One of them always took the duvet and pillow with them in the morning and would sneak into the other one's room. It was usually her.

But one morning she didn't go to him. Instead, she removed the bed linen, packed her things, and took the U-Bahn. She wanted to go far away. He still wrote to her, filled her phone with messages she didn't answer. But when the buds started to burst that spring and the insects broke out of their cocoons, she would still occasionally turn her back on her principles and jump on the U-Bahn to meet him.

She thinks: He was repulsively beautiful that spring. Every time they met. Beautiful. His dark curls highlighting the lovely shape of his head, his green-brown eyes that were all green. He looked like a girl who looks like a boy who looks like a girl. He opened his mouth, and what he said fascinated her. She still wanted to go home, back here, to where he was not.

She turns away from the window. Looks back into the room, into the mess. Longing to go and lie down again, but on the way back to her futon, she stumbles on a cup. Several-days-old coffee runs across the floor, into her calendar. At first, she just stands there, staring at the brown puddle. Then she puts the duvet down, grabs a t-shirt at random from the dirty pile of clothes, and lets it absorb the dirty mess. She picks up her calendar from the floor, uses the hairdryer to dry the pages until they go curly, sharpens a pencil with the eyeliner sharpener, and scribbles today's date until there's a hole in the paper. She writes with big, ugly, almost unreadable handwriting:

Try to change the situation. Regret trying to change the situation. Everything you lose. Imagine if he is right.

She closes the calendar, turns suddenly toward the window again, as if there was someone there. Something. Her hair falls in front of her face, in front of her eyes.

She cannot remember that it was ever articulated as a question, just that Cyril woke her up in the middle of the night with a completely shaved head.

—We'll get married, he said.

At first she was shocked, but to stroke his shaved head was like stroking a cuddly cat. She remembers that he asked her to sit on the stool. Then he got the shaver and removed a stripe of her hair as well. First, like a gigantic part in the middle. Then more and more of her skull appeared. Her eyes grew bigger as her hair fell away, as if from an animal, and the line between head and body became less clear.

—Now we'll be twins, he then said, and afterwards she got under the shower to wash off all the hair that clung to her neck, back, breasts.

Ragnhild drags her fingers through her tangled hair, feels how it reaches down to her bottom now. Then she drags her hands over her cold arms. Goose pimpled skin. She picks up the duvet, wraps it around her again. Looks at her mess, again and again, as if she could find the answer there: in what she brought with her here and how she left him there. Because each time she thinks about it, it changes a little. Now she's trying to remember how important it was to her to wash and tidy after herself, remove all traces. She scrubbed and scrubbed, until she had blisters on her fingers and bruises on her knees. She still kept going. She wanted to make it easier for him to start fresh, after she had left. She opened all the windows and aired herself out of his flat. But when she moved in here, on the other side of town, she just cooped up, sat in the hallway and cried while Tizane tore down the green checkered GDR wallpaper. She wasn't even able to stay properly upright. It was as if she always wanted to be close to the ground. Lie on the floor. All she could think of was Cyril, that it was she who had left and couldn't understand why.

—It's as if you're intoxicated by this pain, Tizane said and pulled her up from the floor, day after day.

Ragnhild pulls a feather sticking out of the duvet. Puts it in the empty flowerpot on the windowsill. When she moved from Cyril, he gave her one of his pot plants, a forget-me-not. After a week, in the shade of the treetop outside her room, it died. Had she told him that? That it dried up? That everything she comes close to, touches, dries up?

She looks down on the floor, on the plate by the futon. She pushes the hairbrush away and takes a bite of the sandwich. She squats, empty eyes, the duvet covering her like a little tent. Suddenly she starts, stiffens. Her phone made a sound. She tries to ignore it. Takes another bite, crunches the bread between her teeth. The phone sounds again. Then she stands up abruptly and finds it on her desk, half-hidden beneath a German dictionary. Nervously presses the green button.

7 November 09.09

(1/2)
I'm really looking forward to
you coming! I feel like a train
that can't stop, a plane that
can't land. I can't wait to brush
the dust from my eyes

(2/2)
and look at you again.
XXX Cyril

She feels the palms of her hands getting clammy. Puts the phone back beneath the dictionary. Just stands there in the middle of the room. From the neighbor's crackling radio, she hears that this will be the coldest winter in a long time, that the snow will cover Berlin like a blanket. She walks over to the basket in the corner of the room, takes a couple of coal pieces and puts them in the stove. Then she tears up an old newspaper and lights it. The flames flare up and die almost immediately. She tries again. Goes down on her knees and blows. Small flakes of ash whirl into her face. She blows a little more before she gives up, throws off the duvet, goes into the bathroom and turns the faucet all the way to the right.

Her white hair has faded. It lies down her back like a dry wheat acre in rainy weather. She picks up the shaving soap and shaver from the shower shelf. Then she begins to shave her legs, her armpits and bikini line, almost mechanically. She pretends that she's doing it for herself, for her own well-being. In the shower mirror she notices that her cheek has a red stripe from her bracelet. She likes it when her skin gets marks from the pillow slip, from the grass, her stockings: she likes that they leave something. That even totally naked you can know what kind of day it has been, what you've been wearing, how you've slept.

She goes out of the shower, dries herself with a rough towel. Then she goes back to her room to get ready. Procrastinates deliberately. Enjoys this moment: Cyril waiting for her. Nervous. Biting his nails. Arranging his curls.

She picks up her makeup purse from the floor and sits down on the futon. Studies her white, straight, characterless teeth in the little mirror in the purse. She used to have a perfect defect once. A crooked front tooth that rubbed itself against the one next to it. It made whistling sounds when she laughed. She has wondered for a long time if she should have the steel string behind them removed, if she should let the lopsidedness come back. She tries to imagine it. A lopsided smile. But all she can see is a thin layer with almost transparent down on her lips. A little boy's moustache. She thought Cyril was making fun of her. But he assured her that it was true, he *was* in love with her almost invisible moustache. He always had to examine her, look at all the details: small light hair over her lips, on her cheek bones, in her nostrils, on her chin. It made her uncomfortable. She is still wondering how he could be so much in love with someone like her, with this almost characterless face, her chubby cheeks and this body of hers with the small breasts, like two unripe apples.

—One day you'll miss the way I look at you, Cyril said once, almost as a warning. And then he added that he would miss how she hit him during the night, in her sleep.

She puts her makeup purse away and walks over to the pile of clean clothes. Finds the gold and black checkered dress, and a pair of pantyhose with ladders down her legs. Puts it on. Changes her mind. Picks up a pair of jeans instead. Tries them on: on and off. Puts her dress and pantyhose back on again. Then she leaves the room, knocks on Tizane's door.

—Come in, she says.

It's warm in there. The coal stove glows and the floor smells of green soap. Tizane puts the accordion down. Ragnhild sits down in the sofa with the cat, strokes its tale, pulls it.

—What do you think, she asks, this dress or these pants?

—Are you really going to meet your husband today? Tizane asks.

—Yes, Ragnhild says.

—Is that very . . .

—No, it's not very sensible, she interrupts, picks up the cat and throws it into the air. Pants or dress, I asked.

Tizane doesn't answer. Aurora slips out of Ragnhild's arms and runs across the floor.

—It'll be fine, Ragnhild says. We're only going to celebrate a bit together.

—Celebrate? Tizane asks and looks at her.

—He was the one who insisted.

—And you?

—I've changed.

Tizane is silent. Doesn't say anything. Ragnhild sighs, gets up and walks towards the door.

—I'll be here when you come back, Tizane says.

Ragnhild doesn't answer, just gives a quick glance then walks into her room. She closes the door behind her, throws the dress on the pile of clean clothes and puts on her jeans. She can hear Tizane continuing to practice the accordion through the wall, as if nothing has happened. As if this is an ordinary day. And perhaps it is, too, for her.

Ragnhild sits down on the floor, her back against the wall, her hands over her ears. This place. This flat. She thinks about the first time they lived together. Tizane was full of energy, full of passion, while she herself was only walking around in her dirty underpants, reading text messages from Cyril. When her mobile bleeped, she started. Felt her back stiffen. And when it was silent, she stared at the empty screen. Just as tensely. She tried several methods, turned down the sound, but then she just walked around pricking up her ears. And when she turned it off, she quickly turned it on again. Just to make sure.

8 June 22.00
I'll never
let you go.

20 July 07.01
I'm not a dog,
I'm a person.

25 July 04.04
You should
talk to a psychiatrist.

7 August 05.44
I feel so empty
without you.
Like a house without
furniture, uninhabitable.

29 August 07.07
Berlin is a city
that has hurt us,
perhaps I'll leave.
Will you come?

8 September 01.22
I've met a woman,
she's nuts about me!
Finally I'm laughing again.

Ragnhild strokes her fingers nervously on the floor, back and forth, feels the unevenness of the wooden planks.

When she received the last text message, she rang Cyril's number immediately. Manically. He picked up the phone, laughed, and asked if she was jealous? And to prove to him that he was wrong, she forced him to tell her. Parker's mouth. Her movements. How she moaned. Every detail. All the way to orgasm. Ragnhild thinks he enjoyed it, her pain, hysteria. That he enjoyed being the strong one. Cyril talked about her muscles. That Parker's muscles are really important. Especially those in her bottom, when she tightens them. And along her arms, her fingers. He told her about the firm grip she's capable of.

She wanted to know what Parker looked like.

—Brown hair, he said. Short. Although she's always trying to grow it. Small body, compact. So everything comes in rapid succession. Tits, bum, and thighs. So you see there are no pauses in Parker's anatomy, he added. Her body is so concentrated that if she'd been smaller, there'd be no room for stimulation. And then the whole point about Parker would've disappeared. Because Parker is physical. She's so intense that it's important to have long gaps between each meeting. Unless you wanted her to exhaust you, he added and laughed again. Yes, actually, he laughed on the phone, through the speaker, then continued: That's why Parker always seems tired and has dark rings under her eyes. Because she has no pauses. From herself. From her enormous sex drive.

Cyril wanted to tell her more, but she stopped him. Turned off the mobile. Lay down on the futon, naked, her legs apart, with the duvet between them. She was scared for the desire to go back. That it would suddenly come over her, like a caprice, like an assault.

—You hurt each other, affectionately, with needles, Tizane said then. Push them further and further under each other's skin.

Tizane got her back on her feet, gave her a paintbrush. Finally she managed to pull herself together, to be helpful, to buy things for their small collective—for the kitchen, the bathroom, the hallway. The only room she left alone was her own: incidental, newly occupied.

Ragnhild looks at the walls. At all the layers that are hidden. Soulless. Her room still smells of paint. She wished they'd kept some of its history, let some stripes of the DDR wallpaper remain. That they hadn't made it so naked, so nice, so obliging. She picks up the nail polish from the floor and begins to paint her nails red. But she can't concentrate. Paints on the outside.

Her things haven't found their own place yet. They lived in boxes for a long time. Boxes that are now folded flat and hidden away. Tizane suggested that she should use them this winter, as firewood. But Ragnhild likes to know that there's room for everything she owns in these boxes. She walked from supermarket to supermarket in his part of the city and collected them. She remembers all the hope they contained. All that freedom in cardboard. And that Cyril looked at them with disgust while she was packing her things in them. Slowly. She didn't want him to know how frightened she was. So she folded her clothes meticulously before she put them away in the boxes: without a system, messily.

—You don't even deserve to have any reminders of me, he screamed.

For the first time he really understood that she was on her way out.

Ragnhild still doesn't comprehend it, his love replaced by hate. All these years together, and then this violent hate.

She taped the boxes, carried them into the hallway. But when he placed himself in front of the entrance door, locked it, she suddenly fell apart. She pulled his arm so hard that his shoulder almost dislocated. Scratched him. Hit out. The skin around his eyes got swollen. So easily. That surprised her. Before she left, she bought him a pair of sooty-colored sunglasses, with large frames and dark lenses. When she visited him a few weeks later, he told her they were his favorite pair.

She breathes heavily, corks up the nail polish bottle and looks out of the window at the grey sky, at the birds flying low over the old communist blocks. No sun in sight. She picks up a pair of woolen socks from the pile of clothes, puts them on, even if the nail polish isn't quite dry yet.

She thinks about all the time that has passed since she met him for the first time: all the seconds, hours, days, months, years, until today. Perhaps he's right after all, that they are like siblings—like twins. Because it was lack of desire that first attracted them to each other, wasn't it? The sexual indifference? Wasn't that what made them so audacious, daring? Because it always had to be something uncomfortable or even macabre to ignite them, like that time she was in the hospital with her arms full of needles, almost unconscious, and he snuck into her room at night and screwed her there, in the hospital bed, next to the flowers from her grandmother and grandfather. He took her hard, her sick body full of anesthetic, while she was looking at the postcards on the night table that he had brought her.

She strokes her stomach with one hand. Tries to breathe calmly. Then she walks over to the window, looks: a village inside the city. A farm girl inside the block of flats. She wonders why this desolate, windblown city landscape has been named after places in Scandinavia. Does it have something to do with the fact that it's so far north, in Berlin? That it may seem desolated and depressing to some? She likes it here, on the edge of everything.

She plucks on a nail in the windowsill. Looks at the buildings on the other side of the street that have holes in the walls, like freckles, she thinks, while she continues to look out over this city that doesn't belong to them. In her neighborhood there are hardly any shops, only Romani who sell their things down there on the empty bus stop: out-of-date travel televisions, car wheels, a yellow-stained pissoir, plastic flowers, a broken wooden carousel horse like the one Cyril wanted when he was a child. For a short moment she wants to put on her boots, run down to the Romani and buy that wooden horse. For him. For their wedding day.

But then she changes her mind. Concentrates on all their arguments again, that claustrophobic feeling, not to forget his laughter full of hate when she moved out, and again, his laughter when she told him all these names in her neighbourhood: Malmöerstraße, Norwegerstraße, Osloerstraße, and Kopenhagenerstraße. It was as if he couldn't stop laughing. Her ears hurt from his gasps, that's how sharp they were. Like broken glass. He thought it was so funny that she didn't manage to get properly away from Scandinavia—only far away from him.

She continues to pick at the nail in the windowsill, lets it scrape off the skin on the tips of her fingers. Outside, the first snowflakes are falling. She pictures Cyril sitting in his flat on the other side of town, waiting for her, curtains drawn, large, yellow, with a crack in between. She thinks: At his place, it's still autumn, perhaps.

She puts her hair in a ponytail and finds her Ushanka hat with the red star at the front that he used to say she looked so good in. Then she goes down to the backyard, unlocks her bicycle, brushes the newly fallen snow from the seat. She could've taken the U-Bahn of course. The U-8 station is just up the road, in a straight line to his place. But she wants to feel the distance: all the streets and buildings that separate them.

She wheels the bicycle out on the road, looks at her tree in front of the block. Tizane is standing in the window up there. She doesn't wave, just stands there and looks down on her. Ragnhild thinks that perhaps Tizane is right, that they don't have any more to say to each other, she and Cyril, that everything has been said, ever since childhood. She still cycles along the slippery, almost white road.

When she's on the red, beautiful, old-fashioned bridge, the name of which she can never remember, which is like an entry to his part of the city, it suddenly stops snowing. She feels the autumn sun on her chin and discovers that she is cycling over rotten leaves. On the farm at home in Bø there was always such a border, a rain border. On one side it was wet, on the other dry. In summer she used to run back and forth in a swimsuit, as if the rain was a gigantic sprinkler for their dry lawn. She often fell and got grass stains on her knees, so that her mother had to scrub her afterwards. She remembers how red and sore she became, how clean. But she has told him that before, too.

She chains the bicycle to the lamp post in front of his block, walks towards the entrance, but then she catches sight of him in the kitchen. He's watering his flowers; the cactus, the paprika plant, the baby tooth moss, and the pansy. She can almost hear him talking to them, these plants that he has named after people in her family. She doesn't want to look at what she likes so much about him, this almost childishness. She's about to ring the bell to the ground floor when the old couple from the floor above comes out.

—Ragnhild, they say, with a strong German accent.

—Herr und Frau Zinecker, she answers and adds: I forgot some of my things. I'm just coming to get the last box. I . . .

She slips into the hallway before they manage to ask any questions. Stands for a while looking at his mailbox. Above her name he's hung a paper note saying: KEINE WERBUNG, BITTE! She straightens her clothes and wipes off the sweat on the palms of her hands. Then she knocks.

Cyril opens almost immediately, as if he's been standing behind the door, waiting. She starts. Stands with one foot in the hall and one inside his place while they politely kiss each other's cheeks.

—Sorry I'm late, she says.

—That's alright, he says, and stares at her mouth, as if he's waiting for her to continue.

She wonders if he still thinks it's charming, this little boy-moustache of hers, now that they're not together anymore.

He scratches his neck.

—Don't you want to come in? he asks.

—Of course.

He shows her inside, as if she was a guest, as if she'd never been there before. She takes off her boots. There's a small hole at the front of one of her woolen socks, so her red toenail shows. She notices that a bit of wool has got stuck to the polish. She pulls the toe in and follows him into the living room. The floor is covered with leaves. Withered leaves from a hanging plant. Like foliage.

She thinks, almost accusingly, that he still likes the autumn best: how the leaves change color, fall from the trees and wither. As if she has hoped for something else. For snow. The fresh, new, white that covers everything.

—You've changed since last time, she says.

—No.

—No?

—You've changed me, he says.

She doesn't answer him. Instead, she notices that there are new things where her things used to be. Smaller things. She studies a glove sewn together by woolen threads with "das Weidenkätzen" written on them. Then she discovers a dandelion with white feathery pappus that he'd put in a small glass cylinder and marked with a yellow Post-it note: Die Pusteblume, it says.

—It's become very nice here, she says, and feels a longing to lift the glass, blow the seeds off. Destroy a bit.

—Thanks, he answers.

Everything in the flat has yellow Post-its with words and gender in German.

—It's really much nicer here now that all my things have been removed, she adds.

He looks away, asks if she wants something to drink, but is already making his way to the kitchen.

She continues to inspect his flat. Walks over to the bookshelf, looks at all the titles. The books are organized by color, size, and genre. Tidy and rigid, she thinks, and notices that he has slipped in a book of comics between Robert Burton's *The Anatomy of Melancholy* and Anaïs Nin's *Incest.*

—Why are you laughing? he asks as he comes back to the living room. He's holding a bottle of Cava and two glasses.

She pulls out the comic book. It's worn, almost falling apart.

—Do you remember the day I skipped sports at high school and ran home to be with you, she says. You were sitting in my parents' basement wearing Mother's fishnet stockings, dress, and pearl necklace. I was watching you for a long time before you saw me. You were smoking menthol cigarettes, drinking cloudberry liqueur, and reading *Calvin and Hobbes*, as if it was the most natural thing in the world.

He pops the cork, fills their glasses, smiles with his lips closed.

—To be with you was always a surprise, she adds.

His mouth changes its shape and suddenly becomes serious.

—To me the biggest surprise was that you left.

She sits down on the sofa, looks at him with eyes full of pity, this look he knows so well which she often hides behind. Then she sips her Cava and rolls a cigarette from his pack.

—You still haven't told me why, he says.

—Why what?

—Why we're not together anymore.

—Cyril, I . . .

—Is it a secret?

—No, of course not.

—So?

She lights her cigarette and pulls deeply, bites her dry lips before she exhales. He stares at her mouth again, but all that comes out is smoke.

—We should get these divorce papers signed, he says then, and leans forward in his chair.

She puts out her cigarette, stands up, walks over to his CD player and presses PLAY. The speakers play piano music. Something classical.

—Do you hear what I'm saying?

She looks out of his window, at the backyard she knows so well.

—I almost bought something for you today, she says.

—What?

—A wooden horse from an old carousel, the kind you wanted when you were a little boy. It was broken, but I'm sure it can be repaired, she says, and turns to him.

—So why didn't you buy it?

—I don't know, she answers and fills her glass with more Cava.

—I dreamt about my child last night, he says, and tries in vain to make her look at him.

—Your child?

—Yes, but when it asked if it had a mother, I had to tell it that its mother disappeared before it came into her tummy.

They are both silent. She takes a long sip. Thinks that she shouldn't drink this early in the day.

—We should've . . .

—Please don't start that again, Cyril, not today. She rolls another cigarette. He's about to open his mouth again, but she stops him.

—Don't, she says, and sucks on her cigarette.

—I thought you'd quit smoking, he says.

—So did I, she says with a small laugh.

He gets up from the chair and sits down next to her in the sofa. He doesn't smell of wet earth after all, she thinks, as he strokes her lightly on the chin.

—Sorry, he says, I didn't mean to . . .

—That's fine, she interrupts and pushes his hand away.

—Can I have a drag? he asks.

She hands him the cigarette. Studies his long fingers with the bitten-off nails.

—You've changed too, he says and gives her back the cigarette. It's wet from his lips.

—Have I? she asks.

—Yes, you look younger, but in a mature way, of course.

—No.

—It suits you.

—What does?

—Your age. I always thought you'd be beautiful as an old woman, he continues. It's just such a pity that I can't share that with you.

She smiles, a kind of sad smile. Slowly changes position, looks at the way he picks up her cigarette from the ashtray. She tries to concentrate on the music, on the notes being played faster and faster, as if the fingers are stumbling over the keys. The piano isn't properly tuned, she suddenly thinks.

—What are we listening to? she asks.

He doesn't answer.

—What are we listening to? she repeats.

—Do you really want to know?

—Yes of course.

He takes a drag on the cigarette. Blows the smoke out of his nose this time. Then, as if he prepared himself, he says:

—It's Parker practicing Beethoven's *Pathétique* at Hanna and Lars's place.

Her body tingles. Small electric shocks of dread, but also signs of arousal: drops of sweat at the roots of her hair, in her armpits, between her toes. She visualizes Parker, how she wakes up Cyril in the middle of the night because she still wants more, licks him everywhere and swallows his sperm when he comes. She thinks about Parker's firm grip. Her smile during orgasm. And Cyril's head between her thighs. His curls that must smell of her sex for days after each visit.

Ragnhild tells him she has to go to the toilet, although she doesn't have to pee, doesn't have to at all. Just sits there pushing. Nothing. Then she buttons up her jeans except for the top button. When she goes to wash her hands, she notices that there are now two toothbrushes in the holder. One of them looks almost new. She opens the cupboard over the washing machine, sees shaving cream, razor, but also pads, moisturizer, and a bottle of perfume, as if Parker is in the process of moving in, she thinks. She sprays a couple of drops on her wrists. But it doesn't smell nice on her. Sweet, like candy. She tries to wash it off. Rubs and rubs until her skin is red and smells of soap. She looks at herself in the polished mirror. Looks away. Tightens the rubber band in her ponytail. Then she flushes the toilet, flushing down: jealousy.

In the hallway she stops in front of the wooden box on the wall. Studies the four small porcelain dolls from the beginning of the last century, without arms or legs or hair, just head and torso, but each with a very different facial expression. Cyril wanted the dolls to represent them: him, her and the two children they pretended they had. She takes one of the dolls. It seems so small lying there in her hand, so brittle. She wants to clench her fist and open it again full of porcelain pieces. Instead she puts it back in the box, somewhere else from where it stood. Refurnishing the concept.

She takes a deep breath and goes back into the living room. There she finds him in exactly the same position as when she left, her cigarette gone out in the corner of his mouth. Evasive, as if time has been suspended.

They're wandering along the canal now, treading on rotten leaves, squinting against the autumn sun. She was the one who finally drove them out of the flat with all her questions about Parker. Indecent, unbearable questions that he answered calmly, and she kept pushing him, until she asked him to stop. His face became distorted and broke into a smile, and then they went outside.

—They've started to cut down the trees along the canal, he suddenly says, breaking the long silence between them.

—Why? she asks.

—It's something about roots, soil, and dams. Something about the trees doing damage to the tourist boats.

She tries to imagine the canal without trees. Like a house without furniture, she thinks, remembering his text message. Then he shows her: trees with their branches cut off so only the trunks are left. Some of the trunks have posters nailed to them showing pictures of how the canal will look stripped bare. They bend over a stump and begin to count the growth rings. She feels a few drops on her neck. Soon after the rain is pelting down, and he opens his big black umbrella. Their bodies brush shyly against each other. She wants it to last, this rain. This smell the rain brings with it. It reminds her of gunpowder, as if nature isn't quite able to swallow everything. She smiles at him while he tells her about the Tree of Ténéré. That there was a solitary tree far out in the Sahara Desert that was drawn on a map and used as a landmark by travelers, and that people took pilgrimages just to look at it. But in the 1970s it was killed by a drunk truck driver. Thousands of years of history, cut down in minutes.

She takes his hand. Soft. It feels as if his thin fingers are curling together with hers, brittle. She thinks how lovely they must've been when he was a baby: tiny baby fingers with even smaller nails. She wonders how it would've looked, this mixture of them. She wants him to stroke her chin again, but she doesn't say anything. Instead, they continue to walk close together under the umbrella. They walk past the boat restaurants floating along the canal. Past the empty areas where people are playing pétanque in summer. Until the tree stubs become trees again, rows of weeping willows. And all the time with this pounding sound of rain over their heads.

Suddenly Ragnhild takes off her ushanka cap and loosens her ponytail so her hair falls down her back.

—Do you like it? she asks and turns to him.

—What?

—My hair.

—No, he says, without looking at her.

He pulls his hand away, picks up a rotten leaf from the ground and pretends to study it.

—I wish we could start afresh, I really do, he continues and throws the leaf back on the ground.

—You can't think like that, she says and puts her arms around him, tries to pull him towards her.

He seems tense, as if he's holding his breath. They continue to walk in silence. She presses him so hard against her that he almost loses his balance. A stray dog limps past them. Barks at the swans in the distance. Then his mobile beeps. She starts, pulls her arms away again. He asks her to hold the umbrella while he looks at his mobile. He gets a strange expression around his mouth, she thinks. He's pressing some of the buttons intensely. A little later his mobile beeps again. She tries to concentrate on something else. An old, frail man is pushing a complaining woman in a wheelchair. She turns to look at them. She's about to open her mouth to say something but sees that Cyril is still busy with his mobile. Finally, he puts it away and looks at her. His eyes look almost empty. She feels an urge to run away. Back to her room. Her things. Curl up on the sofa with Tizane. Lay her head down on her sharp shoulders and listen to her playing the accordion. Stroke Aurora's paws, let the cat's claws scratch her thin skin. But just as she is about to make a sudden move, he stops her, holds her hand hard, as if he understands. Then he takes the umbrella from her. Pulls her against him. She looks away, in another direction, at the skateboard ramp built in the gap between two buildings. A teenage girl is rocking back and forth on her board, without worrying about the cold rain.

—Shh, she says suddenly.

—I wasn't saying anything.

—Shh, she repeats.

—Ragnhild and Cyril, shouts a voice in the distance, like an echo or a memory.

Instinctively, they pull a little away from each other. As if they both felt a strange form of shame for being seen here with the other one. It's a long time since someone has expressed their names in that way, the one after the other, as if they belong together. They stand still, stiff. Like two animals frozen in a particular position when they try to hide. At first, she can't see who's shouting. But then she recognizes Hanna and Lars some distance away.

—Ragnhild and Cyril, they shout again, as their fast steps bring them closer.

When Ragnhild decided to leave Cyril, Hanna and Lars took it as a personal affront. They didn't help her in the least. Neither with packing nor unpacking. Now they're waving enthusiastically.

—Hi, Hanna says breathlessly and gives Ragnhild a hug.

—You're an unusual girl to see in this part of town, Lars says and kisses her cheek lightly.

—Yes, Ragnhild says and blushes slightly.

—It's stopped raining, Lars says and nods at the umbrella.

Cyril puts his hand out, as if to check, before he folds it. Then Ragnhild and Cyril move even farther away from each other.

—Would you like to come with us on Friday? Hanna asks.

—Where? Ragnhild asks.

—To the opening of a new gallery, Lars says. Perhaps we could . . .

—No, Cyril cuts him off, and it looks to Ragnhild as if he almost winks at Lars, and that Lars smiles slightly back.

She feels a stab in the side. It reminds her of the stitch you get when you're running. She picks up a pebble from the ground. Holds it hard in her hand. She's about to ask what kind of gallery they're talking about, but the others are already onto another subject. She looks at them, the others, moving in and out of the conversation. While Lars is telling them ecstatically about David Lynch having just bought Teuffelberg, Ragnhild is thinking about all the fun they used to have together, the four of them. The dinners they cooked, and all the films they watched in each other's living rooms, sofas, and sometimes in each other's beds. She thinks about Parker, too, wonders what Hanna and Lars think about her piano playing, about *Pathétique.* She wants to ask if they think Cyril and Parker suit each other. Instead she listens to Teuffelberg's many stories: from dismantled ski jump, to summer Tivoli, to American monitor station during the Cold War. Apparently, the Ferris wheel had some part in making the signal reception clearer. And now, David Lynch is going to build a university for Consciousness-Based Education and World

Peace, right on top of the small hill where Hitler's war academy is buried, intact.

They turn silent, all four of them. Ragnhild listens to the sounds around them again. The sounds of four small wheels against gravel. She sees the old, frail man from before pushing the still-complaining woman in her wheelchair, this time in the opposite direction.

Then Lars asks:

—Are you coming?

—Where? Ragnhild asks.

—To Teuffelberg of course, Hanna says.

—No, Cyril interrupts. We've got . . .

—. . . plans? Lars asks.

—Yes, Cyril says, it's our thirteenth wedding anniversary today.

Ragnhild and Cyril stand and watch long after Hanna and Lars have disappeared. Then they, too, continue to walk, up a path leading them away from the canal, past a row of occupied houses, as well as a small colony of campervans and trailers.

—Where are we going? Ragnhild asks.

Cyril doesn't answer, pulls her along so her joints hurt, as if he's busy to get somewhere. After a while he stops in front of a rundown wooden house with LINDT CHOCOLATE in neon lights above the entrance. In the window are rows of antique dolls. It takes a little while before Ragnhild realizes it's a shop. Cyril pulls her inside. It's as if the dolls stare at them from everywhere: stacked on shelves, in boxes, some of them are even lying on the floor. They have to tread carefully not to step on them. At the back of the shop, behind a large cash register, a fat old woman is drinking tea from a tiny cup in thin porcelain china. The woman smiles at Cyril in a friendly way.

—Do you want to see them again? she asks.

He nods. The woman puts the teacup on top of the cash register and walks into the back room. Cyril asks Ragnhild to close her eyes. When she opens them again, the woman is holding up a black parcel with a golden bow tied around it.

—Bitte, the woman says and gives it to her.

Ragnhild holds the parcel reverently in her hands.

—Open it when you get home, Cyril says as they leave the shop.

The corners of his mouth are twitching a bit.

—Why? she asks and picks at the tape.

—Because that's when it's going to hurt the most.

Ragnhild is gripping the parcel tightly. Her thumb is boring into the cardboard. She lifts the parcel brusquely. But then she sees the old woman in the shop window. She's standing between all the dolls, waving to them with her fat arms. Ragnhild carefully puts the parcel in her bag.

—It stopped hurting a long time ago, she tells Cyril.

She notices that he becomes silent, that something is happening in his face, a kind of change she can't quite put into words. Then he takes her hand, squeezes it hard, pulls her with him out onto the road and flags down a taxi.

—Einer Kurzstrecke bitte, he says.

Ragnhild opens her eyes. Her body feels beaten up. Her head is pounding. She reaches out for his naked body, but Cyril isn't lying next to her anymore, and she's no longer lying on the floor. Instead, she's lying in a soft, warm bed, on her own. She has no idea why she's wearing his dark-brown suit and his light-yellow shirt with horses, stinking of cigarettes. The last thing she remembers was that he spun her around and around, until they both lost their balance: sliding on the withered leaves on his living room floor. She can't remember how the evening ended. Just that he opened the bar cabinet. And that she mixed everything, with no thoughts of the consequences. A vague sense of intimacy.

It takes some time until her eyes can focus on her surroundings. Then she recognizes Tizane's accordion standing in the middle of the floor, with the bellows half open, like a Japanese fan in red and black. Aurora sharpens her claws against the wall and the charcoal burner glows warmly. Ragnhild is still getting the shivers. She wraps herself in Tizane's duvet that smells of organic cat food and Dr. Hauschka's rose body cream. There's a note on the floor. She picks it up, feeling nervous for a moment.

My dear Ragdoll, it says, in Tizane's handwriting. *I have rose therapy today, so I'll be away for a while. It'd be good if you could give Aurora one of the yellow pills on the desk sometime between two and three. Love, Tiz. PS: If you need something for your headache, you'll find a packet of pills in the bathroom, bottom drawer on the left:)*

Ragnhild folds the note. The winter sun is shining through a small gap in the curtains, blinding her. The branches on the trees outside create neat shadows on the wall. Soon the whole trunk is swaying. She stands up abruptly. Dizzy, she manages to get to the window just in time to see the tree disappear, falling onto the tarmac, as if it lost consciousness. It fills almost the whole road. Soon after men in orange clothing and white helmets start to apply their saws to it. The stump is left, like a gigantic stool. Ragnhild notices that the snowbanks have already begun to get dirty, along the small path by the railway tracks and near the bus stop where the Romani are beginning to pack their gear. She's thinking that the snow doesn't cover the whole town, the way it does in the country, but instead absorbs the pollution, making it more visible.

Passively, she watches the men in their orange suits beginning to load the logs onto a trailer. She wants to shout something nasty to them, but the words get stuck in her throat. So she just stands there, like a rock. Pictures how her tree is going to be cut into small pieces and turned into firewood, burned. Almost like a cremation, she thinks and suddenly feels that it's quite good. The thought softens her. Arms, legs, neck: everything's beginning to move again. Inside her. Because she has always enjoyed funerals. When she was a little girl, she collected insects: everything from spiders to butterflies, millipedes and ants. She trapped them in thin, see-through glasses with long stems, tore off their legs and wings, and lay them carefully in matchboxes full of cotton. Then she picked them up and lowered them down: into a small hole she dug with a spoon on the dry lawn on the farm, where the rain border was. Where it perhaps still is.

She keeps standing like that, naked, staring out of the window. Only when the trailer drives away with her tree does she pull the curtains. She suddenly thinks how different they are, she and Cyril. Because he has never buried anything, killed anything. He even lets mosquitos live.

She lifts Aurora up. Lies down on the bed with this spayed cat that has moved with Tizane to countries all over Europe, but which has never seen anything but flats, always new flats. She loves this cat, which, if it isn't given the prescribed pill before evening would claw itself until it bleeds. She forgives it the ruined bedding, the torn dresses, even the scratched skin. Aurora has never been able to do the ordinary, simple things: mating with a tomcat, walking down the street, climbing a tree or catching a mouse. Now it curls up in her arms. Purrs. Ragnhild pulls the duvet over them both, tries to concentrate on yesterday again, on the holes in her memory.

Cyril had set the table for four late in the evening, wasn't that right? With the dinner set they were given for their wedding, of all things. Because they'd always been so careful with this set, yes, they'd hardly used it. So it remained intact through their whole relationship. Instead, they were the ones who had been chipped, cracked, broken.

Ragnhild strokes the cat's head. Closes the holes in her memory. Everything is streaming toward her now.

She remembers how Cyril pulled the chair so carefully from the dinner table, like a gentleman, so she could sit down. It was as if she witnessed something from the past, something reconstructed. The whole séance had something museum-like about it. Cyril sat down, too. Ceremoniously. The food was delicately arranged on heated plates almost as if they were in a restaurant. And next to them sat the smallest of the porcelain dolls. Cyril clinked his glass, unfolded a tattered piece of paper from the inner pocket of his suit jacket, and performed a long speech, the old speech from their wedding which he'd saved, and then they started to eat. The cutlery made annoying scraping sounds on the plates. And when she chewed, the tender, chewy meat turned to small lumps in her mouth. She tried to get rid of the lumps, wedging them between his books, in the flowerpots, under the cushion on the chair. She doesn't know if Cyril noticed any of it, but he suddenly broke into that laughter of his again and said that her efforts to free herself from him were hopeless, that they were twins, forever, that she might as well give in to it, accept fate, the lines in the palms of her hand. Was it his laugh that was the deciding factor? This passionate yet contemptuous laughter? It was high-pitched, like that of a eunuch. Always this feeling of broken glass when he laughs. Was that why she hit him, again and again? Hit him in the middle of his face, so his nose started to bleed? And then she jumped on him, didn't she? Tore off his clothes and put his prick in her mouth. She remembers the taste of something old, forgotten. Because she didn't know any longer how to hold it in her mouth. It sort of slipped out of her all the time. Was that why she'd tried to imitate Parker, the firm grip she can take? But then he didn't get it up after all. Finally, he asked her to hold firmly around his neck, wasn't that right? That Cyril asked her to squeeze his Adam's apple hard? Push it in. That's when it happened, a certain stiffness in his prick, a small hope before it wilted again. Ragnhild looks at her hands, on the lines inside the palms of her hands. Thinks suddenly that they're frighteningly like his, almost identical. Cyril told her once that you have fate drawn in one and reality in the other, but she can't remember what's what.

The mobile squeaks. Aurora starts and jumps out of bed. Ragnhild reaches for her bag, picks up the phone and nervously pushes the green button. He has sent her a picture, a self-portrait. She studies the small mobile screen. His lips are cracked, swollen, and his eyes are hidden behind the soot-colored sunglasses. Under the picture it says:

Think of me as dead

He hasn't signed it, no Cy, Cyril, or XXX. Just this empty space where his name should've been.

When she puts the mobile back in her bag, she discovers the parcel with the golden bow. She picks it up carefully, holds it in her hand without really knowing what to do with it. Looks at her mobile again. Then she begins to tear off the paper. Inside the parcel is a small box filled with pieces of polystyrene. And among the bits and pieces of polystyrene there's something hard wrapped up in bubble plastic and silk paper. The parcel becomes smaller and smaller as she tears off the different layers. Until she's holding a slender music box. She tightens her jaws. Inside the glass dome is a male doll with painted black hair and silk dinner jacket, while the female doll has long yellow acrylic hair and a pink tulle ballerina dress. She turns the key of the music box with trembling hands. The pair of dolls begin to dance with thin, dangling legs to a tune in a minor key. Their movements are brittle: small, uncontrolled jerks, bordering on collapse.

—Fuck, she says softly to herself. Fuck you.

Tears drip down her cheeks and into her mouth. She turns the glass dome upside-down. Sees how the two dolls now struggle with their movements: their thin legs fall against their heads. She's holding her keys in a firm grip until their movements stop altogether.

She wonders who she is without him. Whether she's become someone else. Or whether she's still the same, just more lonely.

BOILS

Bror is standing in the hallway, looking out of a chink in the curtains. It's raining in the moonlight. It has been raining for many days now; he can't see an end to it. Soon the last snow will be gone. The rotten leaves it covered have started to show again, as well as the mess that was never thrown away. He looks at Judith through the drops on the glass: an unclear picture. She comes walking towards him through the dead avenue of trees, wearing a headlamp and carrying a basket of drenched juniper twigs. He finds himself thinking that soon there'll be as much forest inside as outside. She's walking with firm steps, powerful, as if she owns the place. He's thinking that it's silly of her to be outside in this weather. That she'll get even sicker than she already is. And who'll have to drive her to the hospital then? Wait in bleak corridors?

Once she's out of the avenue, she puts down the basket for a moment and begins to tidy things in the yard: a red rake, a wheelbarrow, a remote-controlled model airplane he crashed into a tree last summer. Wherever she goes, light comes flooding down. He doesn't understand how she can stand carrying on like that. She walks past his steel-grey motorbike, drenched as well. He ought to get it into the garage so it doesn't rust, but he can't bear the thought of running outside in this weather. He takes a sip of his instant coffee instead.

When she picks up the basket again and walks toward the stoop, he quickly closes the curtains, puts the coffee cup on the windowsill and hurries into the living room. Carelessly, he nudges the lopsided Christmas tree so a bauble falls down and breaks. He pushes the pieces under the carpet with his foot, quickly lights a couple of candles. Feels the sweat running under his arms, dampening the light fabric of his pajamas, and sinks down into the armchair, holding the local newspaper, putting his legs on the stool. He flicks through the paper until he gets to the crossword page. Then he lifts the pencil to his mouth and bites it so hard that he tastes graphite mix with his spittle, swallows.

He glances up from the newspaper the moment the door opens.

—Did you have a good walk? he asks.

She takes off the headlamp and proudly holds up the basket, almost loaded with juniper twigs. Several of them have wizened blue berries on them. He wants to say something nice, something that'll make her happy, but then he looks down at the newspaper again.

—You're destroying your eyes in this dark, my dear, she says.

He glances sideways and notices that she walks into the living room without taking off her rubber boots. Small lumps of clay remain on the wooden floor, the rag rug, even the Persian mat. He feels a strange desire to provoke her. Just before her finger reaches the switch, he interrupts her movement.

—It burned out while you were out, he says.

—The bulb?

—Yes, what else?

She shrugs her shoulders, walks over to the chest of drawers, opens a drawer and picks up a new lightbulb. Then she takes the stool from under his feet, stands on it with her rubber boots and changes the bulb. He's blinded by the light when she turns it on.

—Better now? she says and blows out the candles.

He nods, wanting her to stop moving around. She seems to wander around all the time.

—What are you thinking about, Bror? she asks, while she picks up the juniper twigs form the basket and places them in jars around the room.

—Thinking about? He folds the newspaper, puts it on the table.

Nothing. What should that be?

—You seem so distant, that's all, she says.

—Distant?

He picks up the newspaper again, unfolds it and continues with the crossword. He thrusts his jaw back and forth several times as he looks for words. Then he pulls himself together, looks over at Judith. She's about to say something, he can see that from the way she moves her mouth, how her lips become almost round. But at the eleventh hour she opens them again, as if she changes her mind. Wordless and conflict-averse as always, he thinks, while he writes random words in the squares.

—Can't you sit down for a while?

She smiles, her mouth closed, this smile of hers that looks like a large horizontal wrinkle.

—I won't be long, she says and takes off her rubber boots, the red raincoat, the sweatpants, the pantyhose, the underpants with the loose elastic, the woolen singlet and the large bra. Everything remains in a pile on the floor in the hall. He thinks that he should get up and fetch a woolen blanket for her, warm her a little. Yet he remains sitting there. Sunk down in the armchair, he studies her naked body: these yellow boils sticking out from her skin. He looks down at the newspaper again. The words almost flow together, like rain, like storm. He makes little squiggles in the squares.

—What do you want to do later tonight? she asks while she's wrapping her hair, wet from the rain, into a towel turban.

—The same as you, he answers without thinking.

—That's sweet of you, she says and comes over to him. Sits down on the edge of the armchair on her naked bum.

He folds the newspaper again.

—A man isn't sweet, Judith, he's tough or handsome.

—Oh, she says and strokes his hair with her chapped hands that have just been picking junipers, that can pick up dishes from scalding-hot water, that dig the earth.

—Don't we have a good life together? she says and continues to stroke his head.

—Well yes, he says and sits up straighter in the chair. Without thinking, he rolls up the sleeve of his pajama jacket. Scars from old boils are just visible under the new ones. He quickly rolls it down again. A bit of yellow pus is spreading on the inside of the sleeve. He hopes she doesn't notice it. He looks over at the old television in the middle of the room to steer the attention to something else. Like a blind eye, it looks back at him. Dark, empty, speechless.

—*The King's Speech* is on soon, she says. Would you mind defrosting some muffins we can eat while we watch?

—What about dinner?

—That can wait, unless you want to . . .

—No.

He releases himself from her grasp. She didn't hold him with that kind of grasp before, he thinks, and feels his stomach growling. He stands up, walks slowly over to the freezer. He finds the muffins under a wrapped moose-steak with last year's date, takes them out and puts them in the microwave. In the meantime he notices that Judith has taken his place. Making herself comfortable in the armchair, she fiddles with her boils. He thinks with horror about all the bacteria that are rubbed into the material. He hopes she'll manage on her own.

—Do you need help? he still hears himself saying, as he walks toward her.

She looks at him and smiles, showing a row of coffee-stained teeth.

—Yes please, if you don't mind.

She stands up from his chair and lies down on the sofa instead. He bends over her bum and studies it. She has a great bum for her age, he suddenly thinks. A little whore-rump. Almost cellulite-free as well. He feels a tug in his groin. A lust bordering on something else. But then he sits down on his sore knees and begins to squeeze pus out of her boils. A little blood, too. She doesn't scream, doesn't complain, just lies there with a wooden stick between her teeth, like a dog.

—What would I have done without you, she says when he's finished squeezing.

He doesn't answer, walks over to the basin, holds his fingers under water as hot as he can take. Washes himself thoroughly, the way he learned when he was a child.

—How are yours? she asks and stands up from the sofa.

—Well, they're just there, he answers and notices how the hot water burns him.

—Do you need help? she asks and walks towards him.

—No, he says and dries his fingers on the apron hanging on the hook. No, he repeats.

She shrugs her shoulders.

—Just let me know, she says, and takes the muffins out of the microwave and puts them in the oven. Then she walks over to the hall, fetches a pile of clothes from the wardrobe and spreads them across the floor.

—What do you think? she asks.

—About what?

—The dresses, silly.

—They're all just as nice, he says without looking at them.

They hear fireworks in the distance. The sounds are like a thunderstorm.

—Oh no, Judith says and pretends to hide her face in her hands. Why do they start so early, Bror?

When she's worried, he thinks her foreign accent is more prominent. For some reason, it amuses him.

—Let them keep at it, he says. Nothing can happen as long as I'm taking care of you, he adds, with an unexpected pride in his voice.

She smiles stiffly at him, a kind of brave smile, and pulls sheer nylon stocking on her thick legs. Every time a rocket is fired, she still starts. These small jerks in Judith's body. Like a remote-control doll, or a model airplane. He looks past the boils, the varicose veins on her legs, the stretch marks on her hips—like small twigs on a tree, he thinks, and can't help liking them. Between her navel and her sex she has a scar she has refused to tell him about. She just arrived, without history, but with marks.

—I love you, he says suddenly.

Judith stops for a moment, looks at him with big eyes, her body halfway into a dress.

—It's important to dress up for each other on a day like this, she says.

He doesn't answer, walks over to the fireplace, puts in a new log, the last in the basket. Then he sits down in the chair, erases the squiggles in the crossword and starts again. He tries to concentrate. From time to time, he throws a quick glance up from the newspaper to see how she puts on airs with her different dresses.

—Do I look nice now? she asks, while wriggling her hips and pouting.

—Why don't you sit down, he answers.

She sits down on the sofa. Sits there with her legs clumsily crossed. An effort to look elegant, he thinks. They sit in silence and stare into the flames for a long time. Or out of the window, at the fireworks in the distance. Then she starts to talk again.

—Isn't it strange, she says.

—What? he asks, surprised.

—That someone else's childhood, sweethearts, life, can become entangled with your own history and mean everything.

—Yes, but . . .

—Imagine if we should break up one day, Bror.

—Judith, he says firmly, almost angrily.

She waits for a while, but that's all. She continues as if he hadn't said anything.

—And your parents that I know so well, she says, and the place where you grew up, the townhouse in the city . . .

—Let's talk about something else, he interrupts.

She becomes silent, but he still refrains from asking questions.

He can feel it rubbing against him, all these things she knows about him. Why couldn't he have kept his mouth shut, like she did?

He knows almost nothing about her life before she came here. A childhood picture was all she showed him. And that's more than enough, she had said. She, who knows almost everything about him, had said that's enough questions. And he doesn't know why, but he avoided pushing her.

Suddenly he thinks that he's almost a bit happy about that. Because if she were to disappear, all she'd take with her is the time they'd had together. No shared memories of earlier years.

Apart from this one childhood picture, that is, of a girl in a field; a rock in her hands, golden corkscrew curls sticking out from her scarf. It suddenly strikes him that the child in the photo might not be Judith, the way he has always believed, but a total stranger.

He looks at her again. At her grey, almost white hair. She's colorless, like the buildings in Eastern European countries. He thinks again that if she should disappear, perhaps no one would miss her.

He can see that she's uneasy. At first he thinks that it's because of the fireworks, but then he realizes that she's staring at him. It's an uncomfortable feeling.

—It's getting worse and worse, she says.

—What is?

—The boils, of course. It's as if it'll never be over. Perhaps we should go to the doctor again?

—No, he says.

—Why not?

He doesn't have an answer for that. Just stares into the flames, as if he can find an answer there in what's burning and slowly dying down.

—It was you who gave them to me, he says instead.

—That's what you think, she says.

He doesn't answer that either.

—Anyway, what does that have to do with it?

He can't stand the thought of the bleak corridors, not again. He feels an urge to stand up and smack her face. Watch her porous skeleton fall to the floor. Smolder. Become dust again.

—It'll pass, Judith, he says. Everything has an end, he adds, after a while.

They sit in silence. The fireworks in the distance. The dying flames in the fireplace. Then her eyes move to the log basket.

—It's empty, he says and gets up. His movements sluggish.

—Are you getting more? she asks.

—No, he answers, shuffles over to the kitchen bench, opens the top drawer and finds some Christmas napkins. Then he bends down and wipes up the traces of mud she has left.

—I'm just going to the loo, he says and throws the dirty napkins in the embers.

He almost steps on some of her clothes as he opens the door to the bathroom. Then he closes it and sits down on the toilet lid. He sits there and thinks about the time before he met her: when he was working out on the North Sea, saving money for a place like this. Every time he had a day off, he would drive from farm to farm on his motorbike, searching. He'd almost given up when he found this ramshackle place. Bought it. He remembers how it looked when he first came here. The house was decayed and had to be pulled down. The yard was full of junk that had to be thrown away. Wrecked cars in the garden, old porno magazines in the barn. But he got rid of it all and rebuilt the farm from the bottom up. And the day everything was done, the day he painted the final coat, Judith arrived. Yes, that's really how it was: she just happened to pass by with a small grey backpack. She said something about having got lost. She didn't speak Norwegian all that well then, not like now. He asked her in for a cup of coffee, which became a beer, which became a glass of moonshine, perhaps a few, and then she never left. She opened her backpack carefully, put her few clothes discreetly next to his in the wardrobe, took out a bible in an unintelligible language, put it in the night table drawer and made the unoccupied space in the double bed her own. He almost didn't notice. How she slowly but surely took more and more room, made herself at home. What happened to him in all this? He suddenly feels tears pushing against his eyelids. He sits and sobs on the toilet lid as quietly as he can. Swallows the sounds.

—Hurry up, Bror, he hears her shouting. The King's arriving!

He dries his tears, looks in the mirror. A feeling of nausea spreads through his body. A kind of fear, maybe. How did he get to look like this? His face is so swollen that he barely recognizes himself. It distorts him, distorts his expression. A boil on the top of his cheekbone pushes his cheek so high up that his eye almost closes. One inside his nostril makes his nose larger. Full of pus. He squeezes the right wing of his nose gently, but it hurts so much that he quickly stops. They'll just have to be there, he thinks and instead combs his hair as far as he can over his face. Despondently he looks at the brush full of grey hair. He opens the lid and throws it in. Stands for a while and looks down on the grey wisp of hair in the golden toilet, floating in the water. Looks at the golden mirror, the baroque bathtub too. He vaguely remembers a desire to make something elegant in this rustic environment. Perhaps he should dress up a little? Take off his pajamas and polish his shoes? That'd make Judith happy. But then he looks at his watch, sees how late it is already. He pulls the chain and opens the door.

—. . . *We must be able to look at ourselves in the mirror each morning and say that we're trying to be the best we can*, he hears the King saying from the small screen.

The best? Bror thinks. What the hell does that mean? For a short moment he stands in the hallway and studies all the things she has bought with his money since she moved in here. Besides the gaudy Christmas finery that'll soon be put back into boxes, stowed away, forgotten, she has got herself porcelain knickknacks. Plastic dolls. Even a picture of the previous pope, which she bought at the flea market down in the village and hung above the sofa, without even asking him what he thought. Before she came into his life, there were no sentimental items here. No decorations. Only his motorcycle magazines and hunting rifle. Then it was easy to keep the house tidy, he thinks, stepping over her pile of wet clothes and sinking down into the armchair again. Then he notices that Judith has put on the flowery summer dress he gave her for Christmas. He can see that she's cold. It looks as if the small hairs on her upper arms are standing straight up, like rushes in the ocean. And the side zipper is only half-zipped. She looks like a stuffed animal, he thinks and is ashamed.

—You look very nice, he says and takes one of the warm muffins Judith has put on a tray.

—Thanks, she says and holds out her clammy hand.

He hesitates for a moment before he takes it. Holds her stubby fingers carefully, one of them with a golden ring.

—I think that growing as a human being also means to dare to meet challenges, to stand for what we believe in, the King says.

To grow as a human being, yes, Bror thinks. He looks over

at Judith, who only has eyes for the King just now. He lets his eyes roam, to the bridal photo in the golden frame on the top of the television set. It's as if it wasn't him and Judith, but two strangers, a pair of happy people from another world, another time.

—Judith, he says suddenly, clearing his throat.

—Yes, darling? she asks, her eyes still on the screen.

—There's something I have to tell you.

—Hmm . . . what?

She takes a muffin, too. She picks out the raisins with her free hand and puts them on the table.

—I want to be by myself a little more, he says.

The silence falls around him like a sweater with a too-tight neck, itching. She pulls her hand slowly out of his, turns off the sound on the television and looks at him with surprise. He doesn't know what to do, picks up the raisins she has put on the table and puts them in his mouth.

—Why don't you take your bike out for a ride, she says after a long pause.

—In this weather?

—Surely you don't mean that I should go out again?

—No, that's not what I meant.

—What did you mean then? she asks and tries to make eye contact.

—Perhaps it isn't all that important after all, he says and concentrates on the screen. Sees how the King moves his mouth without a single sound coming out of it.

—Was there something else you were going to say? she asks.

—No, he says, no, I don't think so.

He gets up, walks over to the fridge and takes out the six-pack that's hidden behind the turkey.

[illegible] you want one? he asks instead and opens a bottle.

—Why do you ask when you know I've stopped drinking?

He doesn't answer, just takes a long swig, wraps himself into a blanket.

The words from before are as if erased, withdrawn. Just a queasy smell is left, a smell of something burnt, of ash. Now the King's words fill the room again. Bror sits down in the armchair. Sits there and drinks. Doesn't know what else to do.

He misses the time when they could share a drink. The two of them, drinking themselves silly. He felt such a closeness to her then, such a responsibility. And she almost always started to cry. He liked that, too, her swollen eyes and her very white, very thick tears, almost like breast milk. He enjoyed comforting her, it made him feel, well, useful or something. And he didn't mind that she talked to him in that unintelligible language of hers. Rather the opposite, he enjoyed it, that he could fill her words with whatever he liked.

—My experience is that we rarely regret what we have to do to push ourselves to dare doing. It is often what we never did, that we regret, the King says.

Bror stands up from the chair, walks toward the hallway. Judith doesn't look at him once. Doesn't try to stop him. He puts on the headlamp, opens the front door and walks into the rain in his socks, like an obstinate little boy. His socks get drenched immediately. His hair and clothes as well. He feels the water running down his back. It almost feels nice. As if it cools down the pain from the boils, soothes it. His headlamp lights the way to his motorbike. His silver-grey and wet Ducati. He sits on it. Just sits there. How could he have forgotten it, this life on the bike? Endless roads. Alone. Turns almost causing a fall. All he sits on now is his armchair. His fat bum sunk down into it. A face he no longer recognizes. That he can't love. Not even Judith can love this face, he thinks. She's lying. She's lying because she hasn't got anywhere else to go. That's why she's clinging to him.

He has no idea how long he remains sitting there in the rain before he goes back in. He takes off his headlamp in the hall, his wet pajamas, the boxer shorts Judith gave him for Christmas, and his dirty socks. Let it all just lie there, on top of her wet clothes. Naked, he walks over to the stairs without looking at Judith, without looking back. Along the passage to the bedroom, where his motorcycle helmet and leather uniform are hanging. He lets his fingers glide over the solid surface, hard. He likes to wear clothes that are a bit firm, jeans, leather or something. It's as if he needs something hard to hold himself up. He takes the leather uniform off the hanger. Puts it on with nothing underneath. Leather against skin. Padded knees and elbows. Puts on the helmet too. Gets a glimpse of himself in the window before he sits down on the edge of the bed. He sits there, on the clean and freshly ironed bed linen Judith has put on for the occasion. He looks at the moose antlers hanging above the bed, decorated with Christmas tinsel. Then he stands up, walks over to the weapon cupboard that has been locked for more than a year now and turns the key. Inside the cupboard is his hunting rifle. He almost becomes touched when he sees it. Suddenly remembers all the wild moments they've shared, the two of them. He takes the rifle from the stand, holds it in his arms. It surprises him how light it feels. He picks up the ammunition, puts the cartridges in the magazine, one by one, until it's full. Then he goes through the loading motions and walks silently down the stairs.

—*I wish you all a happy new year*, the King finishes.

Bror pulls the trigger. Hardly takes aim. Doesn't stop before the rifle is empty of cartridges and Judith is full of holes. Like a battlefield of craters in her body, he finds himself thinking as the blood is pumping out of the flowers in her dress and down onto the floor. Some of it runs in a small stream towards him. He feels her warm blood against his bare feet. Takes a step to the side. Then he puts the rifle calmly on the table, pulls off his helmet and looks over at Judith again. She has totally collapsed now; a wrung-out rag. He tries to pull her upright again. But when he lifts her head, she looks at him with her large eyes. Glazed. Empty. He lets go. Lets her fall. Opens a new bottle of beer. Takes a big sip. Then he sits down in the armchair. Sits there in his motorcycle uniform. Old rain and fresh sweat runs down his face, mixes with the smell of gunpowder and blood. He looks at the television, but the pictures on it just glide through him without leaving a single trace. He thinks for a moment that perhaps he should turn it off. He could. Instead he sinks further and further down into the armchair. Now and then he looks out of the window. It's still raining. It looks like it'll never stop. Tonight, the rain's good, he thinks. But tomorrow I'll scream if it continues.

MONITOR

I swear, the bags under my eyes are like blisters. I should lance them. They distort my face, my eyes, they keep me awake. I've stolen needles from the factory. A little blue box of sewing needles. I squeeze the bag under one eye. Just a cigarette first. I take deep puffs; blow rings. A last cigarette before breakfast. Just one. Then I'll squash the packet so the cigarettes break in the middle. Throw it at the wall. I count the stubs in the jam jar. The ones with red lipstick marks don't count. The ones with pink lipstick marks don't count either. Still. My pores open. I notice how my skin grows coarser, my thoughts as well. I put out the cigarette on the back of my hand. As punishment. Kunyaza, kunyaza . . .

I swear I can hear someone standing right outside my window, biting their nails. I squeeze the bag under one eye: as if it were only a bit of pus in my delicate skin, then I take the little blue box from my sock. I'm shivering, the needle between my fingers. I insert it, prod my skin, make small, imprecise holes, carelessly, as if the bag under my eye was a needle cushion. Then the skin finally breaks and the needle is sticking straight out. Insert a needle in the other eyesocket too. There. Now it's good.

My head feels weightless and metallic. The room suddenly smells sweet. Almost like sperm. Until I blink. Several times, consecutively. Involuntarily. The needles fall out: useless, insensitive antennae. I try to insert new needles, prodding the holes, widening them, but my skin refuses to obey.

I remember: my nerve-endings. The sunlight as a stripe on the wall. A reindeer staring into the headlights. I remember the light of the cigarette glow.

I press my face against the wall. Let it rest a little against the concrete. Cold. Then I slowly move across. The surface scrapes my skin, like an unshaven man. I stop, stare into a socket. Attracted by the two dark holes.

Criminal Code § 201 letter b.

It is proven that the accused surveyed her ex-boyfriend while she lived in the flat as well. She was sitting in an adjoining room watching the offended on a monitor.

Wait, an insect: the sound of my eyelashes beating against each other. Of the sweat running under my hair, my armpits, between my toes. Of my breath when I'm holding it. I swear, when you're alone, I mean . . . Forget it. I have to forget it. I mustn't have any feelings. No no no. I could become randy. Have to become randy. But no feelings. Not here. And I usually don't pick up the phone when someone calls. Not usually. Forgotten.

I swear, I can hear the hair growing on my legs. You can see the beginning of a few red pubic hairs near the waistband. I push in a finger. Look around, can't see anyone. Feel absence. I don't understand why it doesn't work anymore. It should work. I want to masturbate myself blind. Try it. Masturbate myself stupid.

Retarded. Just by rubbing, just by pushing in a finger. Rotating it. Rotating. Tighten all my muscles to the point of exhaustion. Lay my head back, half-open my mouth. Imitate ecstasy. Nevertheless, nothing, nothing, just the sound of my own choices. The bones in my body snap like an old tree. And the holes in my skin feel like insect bites.

I scrape my nail against the walls of my vagina. Dry. Pull the finger out of the hole. Put it in my mouth instead. It tastes of dust. Of dirt. Of having touched the floor too much.

Oh no. I swear. Not to be wet. I'd rather go to the toilet and put water on my cunt.

There'll be problems when they find out. Big fucking problems.

I'm tired. It's just the body that doesn't want to; it needs rest. I never used to be dry. Then I did it with the light on. All the lights. Even the neon light above his sewing machine. And then I photographed my sex with a polaroid camera. Sent it to an incidental name in the phone book. Perhaps I should tell someone?

I have to open the window. Let in some fresh air. Not pull the curtains. Not work against myself.

The accused surveyed the offended with the help of three cameras that wirelessly transmitted photographs to the monitor. She continued to survey him after she had moved out.

I pull a hair from my head, thread it through the eye of the needle. Sewing. I swear, I could sew a prick to my cunt-lips. Blindsiding. I love the sound of things like that. Insects like that.

Wait, someone that . . . I put my finger into my pants again, rub, rub, the pink nub at the very top. Perhaps it helps to talk about it?

A cockroach scuttles across the floor, just touching my big toe. I catch it, pressing it into the wall. Hold it there. Suck my fingers, rub them on my clitoris. Fast. Feverishly. All these thoughts. Let them relax while I rub. Like taking out the plug in a bathtub filled with water, or when clogged ears suddenly pop. But it doesn't work. Nothing works anymore. I stop. Press the cockroach even harder against the wall. Discharge oozes out, and the sound I hear reminds me of eating crisp bread.

Criminal Code § 201 letter b.

The accused has admitted that she placed a hidden camera in a decoder in the living room of the offended. Later she placed another hidden camera in the flat, this time on a television in the guest room. For Christmas the same year she gave the offended a television for the bedroom. A hidden camera was installed in the television.

I want to unstitch the seam, the one holding the scrotal pouch together, take the needle and tear up the balls, stitch by stitch, until all the insects inside trickle out. Is it going to happen now? The contractions of the cunt muscles? Cramp?

No, not now. Not that. All right then.

I'm biting my nails. I have to get my blood to circulate. Through my whole body. Get it to swell up, make my thoughts disappear. I get a mirror. A small cunt-mirror in a golden frame. I sit down on the concrete floor, spread my legs, study my grey cunt. The batwings. The lips trying to fly. I take thorough steps. Have to find a kind of method. I know of a Central African tribe that teaches their children how to cause a female ejaculation. Ejaculation? That's right. Kunyaza, kunyaza, kunyaza.

The accused has until recently worked as a seamstress in a factory, but has now lost her position because of redundancy. She claims that she obtained the monitoring equipment to have something to do.

Alone at home in his home. My cunt, that's where I started it: heavy, dusty books. Old. With pages almost as thin as the skin under your eyes.

"The female sex consists of the outer labia (where hair is growing) and the inner labia. The head of the clitoris is, like the male penis, built up of erectile tissues that become filled with blood when stimulated, making the sex swell up. The clitoris is larger than earlier supposed, actually as big as a medium size penis. Its only function is enjoyment and pleasure."

Its only function is fiction. Exactly.

Criminal Code § 201 letter b.

The accused has admitted that she watched the monitor three or four times a day.

I can't see clearly in this cunt-mirror. The beat of the batwings. The egg that slides out. But I swear that I can hear it.

However, it could not make recordings.

They say I have an illness embedded in the clitoris, or somewhere in the erectile tissues.

The Court of Appeals has accordingly arrived at the conclusion that the accused has shown a sexually offensive or other indecent behavior, especially towards the offended, but also towards others she has observed in erotically charged situations on her monitor.

A mosquito lands on my cheek. Another on my other cheek. I hit out. I slap them. Something must burn in order for it to become light. I swear, I can see the bones in my body as if in an X-ray; I can see things from the back of my head. I can . . . No.

I find the tweezers I've hidden in my shoe. Begin to pluck the hairs that grow on my legs, like weeds. I have to clean up my act, put things straight.

I crawl under the bed, get a dust bunny that's hiding there. I'm about to throw it out of the locked window, but then I get an idea. I want to take it for a walk here in my room. I give it a name: the letter b. Benny. After a while, it gets tired and wants to lie on the windowsill. Join an offshoot from a plant in a cutoff plastic flask with a bit of bark and soil. It stretches toward the sunrays that force themselves through the dirty window. It smells nice when you rub your fingers on the leaves. Like sweat in the armpits, between the legs, under the scrotum.

Perhaps it would calm me down if I bite off my clitoris, embroider a tablecloth with dead nerve endings from my sex?

Wait, I think I hear a sound, almost like my eyelashes when they beat against each other. Something tickling. The hairs on my skin stand up. I feel a shadow under my skirt. I swear, it has to be cockroaches. They're creeping up my thighs and into my hole. I lay my head back. Squeeze my legs together. Draw my eyes up, down, in, out, rotating them, drawing them to the sides. Repeating these movements again and again: up down in out. I hear nails against a blackboard. Forks against glass. The blood disappears from my ears and makes me dizzy. Then I feel a lifelessness and sticky mass between my thighs. Open up to something crushed and bloody: a scar on my white skin.

Criminal Code § 201 letter b.

A person who undertakes something as unusual as installing hidden cameras in someone else's apartment has a duty to check beforehand whether this is legal.

I apply pink lipstick, pick up the squashed packet of cigarettes from the floor and light a broken cigarette. Those with a red edge don't count. I blow smoke out of my nostrils. No other sound in the snail house. I take one puff after the other, then I put out the cigarette on the floor, lie down on the bed and pull the duvet over me. Hands on top of the duvet, my grandma used to say. I put them on top of the duvet. Pick at the yellow grain that has gathered in the corner of my eye, like dust. Study my nails: rough, small. I think about all the dead skin I'm carrying. All the dead cells. A couple of kilos, I read somewhere. Then I feel something warm running between my legs. The sheet draws the urine into it and gets a nice yellow color. I let it run. It's so good to lie here. I think I need rest.

I stroke my forehead, warm, pull out an eyelash. One for each day. If an eyelash loosens on its own, I can wish for something. If there's something I would like to wish for, it's to get my monitor and the three cameras back.

REPEAT AD LIBITUM

Cuts his hair. Bristly, a bit dry. Away from his eyes. Regrets it. Buys a wig, cuts it. Gets a glimpse of himself in the mirror wearing the wig. Looks away. Down. Breaks the mirror, keeps the wig, puts Band-Aids on his hand. Opens the wardrobe and looks at all Nusch's dresses. Chooses one he thinks suits her best, one he gave her. Takes it off the hanger. The dress has a sweetish smell, almost sickening, a bit like formula. He tears it up. He has often dreamed of torn dresses, but now he's disappointed. The feeling did not meet the expectations. Still, he continues. Systematically, working through her wardrobe: cuts off buttons, sequins, and zippers. Cuts her hats to pieces as well. He doesn't even spare the national costume shirt she herself embroidered with roses. While he's picking at the threads with his long, messy nails and rips the roses off, he looks out of the chink of the door: through the hallway, over to her piano in the living room. It just stands there without making a single sound. He quickly stands up, closes the door. Then he continues the laborious work. The shirt of her national costume has a large brown stain on the chest. He wonders how she could hang it up in the wardrobe like that without washing it. He cuts out the stain.

He remembers insignificant things that suddenly move something inside him. Things that irritated him. The way he often found her in the kitchen, her fingers fumbling inside the coffee container. He thought it was dirty, but he never dared to tell her. She made coffee all day long. She said it was because she liked how the smell permeated the house with a fresh kind of bitterness. And all that coffee, what was she going to do with it? Usually, the cup was next to her on the living room table, untouched. She claimed that this became a metronome for her: back and forth, to and from the kitchen. That it gave her a kind of rhythm in her life, a direction. What could you say to something like that? Get a job! Talk to someone at the old people's home. Change a diaper. Plough the earth. Plant potatoes. Learn an old craft!

He throws her national shirt on the floor. It has a large hole in the chest and no more embroidered roses. He's proud that he finally dared to tackle something meaningful to him. The feeling of destroying, the freedom of it, excites him. He lifts the bridal dress she inherited from her mother, who inherited it from her mother, down from the hanger. Takes it out of the plastic bag, cuts the thick silk up into thin strips, almost like confetti. Cuts and cuts, until his fingers are sore. He puts the scissors down for a moment and discovers that he's about to get two large blisters between his thumb and index finger.

He looks at the mess he's made. Walks over to the window, looks out: the street: no traffic. Just a row of cars that have been parked there for so long that they've started to rust. And the boys bungee jumping over by the garbage heap. Behind them: the concrete block of flats casting a shadow for the sun, dish antennas sticking out of almost all the balconies, but no other people in sight. He pulls the curtains, relieved. Takes off his wig, puts it in the wardrobe, on top of the now empty hat shelf. Looks once more at the mess he's made. Collects the pieces of the broken mirror. Sees checkered images of himself: in the garbage bin. Picks up the buttons, zippers, and all the tiny sequins from the floor and puts them in clean yogurt containers. He neatly folds the strips of material, and puts them in four cardboard boxes with *summer, autumn, winter, spring* written in felt pen on the lids. He goes through all the drawers, shelves, and baskets around the house. Only her piano is left untouched. He carries the rest of her things into the box room, closes the door.

The first time Nusch left him, he cried and thought he'd never see her again. The second time he felt insulted and didn't want to see her again. The third time, he cursed her, slammed the door, and waited for her to come back.

He can't sleep. Lies on the sofa in the living room and looks at the silent piano. Looks at the keys, black and white. Several of them are cracked. On some of them, the white has flaked off, revealing the brown color underneath, as if she had spilled coffee on them. He suddenly sees her in front of his eyes, sitting there on the old piano stool, coffee cup in one hand, music book in the other.

Once, just before she left, she was sitting there leafing through the music as if she was reading a book. Always the same pages, always *Für Elise am 27. April zur Erinnerung von L. v. Bthvn.* Back and forth until the sheets ripped. Now they're held together with tape, these notes that everyone in her family has had to learn: mother, grandmother, great-grandmother, only never to come near the piano again. No one got further than *Für Elise*. Not Nusch either, she stagnated there, like a record with a scratch in it, he thinks. Stands up and tears the music book to pieces. He's almost surprised at how easy it is to tear up. Collects the pieces and locks himself in the closet room with her things.

Nusch is the type to seem genial in her absence, he thinks. It's as if everything else, everyone else, pales in comparison. No one can be absent in a better, more refined way. How she refuses to answer the phone when he rings her, the silence after he has posted a letter. Only when he's totally broken does he believe she'll come back to him. And slowly but surely, perhaps everything will be the way it was before she left. Immobile. And in a strange way, he's looking forward to that: to be able to relax a little again, in bed with her.

The days pass, but still not a word from Nusch. Instead, he constantly stumbles into her piano, on his way to and from the living room. But he's the only one it hurts.

Early one morning he rents a trailer. He coaxes a gang of teenagers hanging out near his house, worn backpacks on their shoulders, to come over. Gives them cigarettes, booze, and old porno magazines. The dirty teenage hands lifting the heavy piano out of the doorway and onto the trailer move something in him. The stink as well, from rotting garbage. It's as if the smell has got stuck to their rough clothes, disheveled heads, fresh cheeks, their very minds.

When everything's on the trailer, including the teenagers and the piano stool, he drives recklessly up the hill, afraid of meeting anyone. But the street remains empty, as if there was no one else living here but him and his load. The teenagers toss the piano into the huge garbage dump; he throws the piano stool after it. Now he can't bring himself to watch this any longer, this massacre he himself has organized. He thanks the teenagers and hurries off.

When he has returned the trailer, she suddenly rings.

That evening he sits facing Nusch in a dim bar. Despite soaking himself in the bathtub for hours, and spraying himself with aftershave, he can still feel the garbage stink clinging to him. He steals glimpses of himself in the neon-lit bar mirror. Notices his skin: blue-white and wrinkled, like that of an old man. He looks down. Can't bear to meet his sharp, pitiless gaze. His cheeks itch because of the aftershave. He hopes she doesn't find him repulsive. He lifts his eyebrows. Thinks that he probably has this surprised expression every time Nusch comes back. Because he can't get used to it. Get used to her. Or to her skin: white as chalk and ghostlike, almost transparent. She has tied a yellow shawl over her head and her eyes are black with eyeliner, like a dirty river on the waterline.

—You look like someone else, he says. Someone I recognize without quite being able to identify.

Perhaps he's talking about himself. His voice is hoarse. He hasn't used it all that much lately.

—What? she asks.

—Nothing, he says. Nothing, he repeats and takes her hand.

Her fingers are bony, cold. He tries to warm them between his legs. The bar is dark and the music is loud. He wonders if perhaps that'll take away the pressure to talk to each other. At first they drink more than they talk, listening to the rhythms of the room: steps coming, steps going. But it never quite fills up, this place. It was Nusch's choice to meet here. It's a test, he thinks, she brings me to a place I'm so obviously not going to like. He smiles at her impudence. They order more drinks. After a while her cheeks turn red and her eyes blank. She is the one who's trying to talk now. She's saying something he can't quite catch. Instead, he notices something strange in her voice. It hasn't occurred to him before that she speaks with an odd kind of accent. Not an accent, exactly, but something foreign, with a small hint of deafness, maybe. Her lips, and the sounds coming out of them, are in a funny way not quite in sync, as if she's dubbing herself.

—Are you listening? she asks.

He nods. Discovers that she's talking about his hair. She's commenting with a smile that it gets shorter and shorter whenever they're apart. And she seems to think that it suits him, this short hair, that it makes him more manly in a way, more mature. What she means by that, she doesn't quite know herself, she says. Still, he'd like to thank her for the compliment. He opens his mouth with the best of intentions, but it comes out as something else, something that makes her cry. He doesn't understand it. Tries to dry her tears. They're running down her cheeks. He finds a handkerchief. It's crumpled, used. She looks gratefully at him, blows her nose in a clean corner of the material while he studies her swollen face, red nose, sore eyes with the mascara smudged across her face. He always thought that her tears looked good on her, that they add life to her face.

—Why did you come back? he then asks, almost angrily.

—I don't know, she says. I just thought we could . . .

He waits for her to finish the sentence, but it just hangs in the air. Instead, she excuses herself and goes to the toilet. She always has to do that, go for a pee. While she's away, he thinks about all the boxes stacked in the box room, the piano and the stool in the garbage dump, everything he has destroyed. She's away for a long time. He tries to let the music drown out his thoughts. Orders another drink. Looks out on the empty dance floor.

—Perhaps the best thing about leaving is to come back, she suddenly whispers in his ear.

She came back without him noticing. Now she's sitting next to him again. Her bony hands on his neck. How could she say something like that? Something so spot on. Her eyes are placed very far from each other, almost like on a fish. He's heard you can get that kind of eyes if your mother drinks too much during the pregnancy. He's about to say something nasty, something he knows will hurt her, but instead he's being pulled out onto the empty dance floor. At first he protests. Still has all these nasty words on the tip of his tongue. But then he gives in. Drops the words. While they're dancing, he holds her very hard to stop her from falling, and her dress is bunched up around her bottom. Her legs are shaking. She seems to have been thinking about this for quite some time, if she should come back or not, yet again.

They throw Nusch out just before closing time. He follows her. Together, they stagger back to his place, to their place, past plains with dead grass and dishwashers and fridges thrown on the scrapheap. Past the stink from the garbage dump where old furniture and rotten food have been thrown over her piano. Past the blocks of discarded satellite dishes. Past all these things she's been missing, she says, and he believes her. Every time. They're coming closer. He looks at his rundown house from a certain distance this time, looks at the cement sheeting covering the facade. Several of the sheets are broken, have fallen off. Now they're suddenly standing there again, her bony hands in his, in front of this postwar house where Nusch moves in, moves out, and moves in again. Just as it suits her. And he lets her keep doing it. Because in a strange way he likes this draft.

Someone has drawn a hopscotch in chalk on the sidewalk, which the weather has almost wiped out. He takes the keys from his pocket and throws them down on the hopscotch in front of him, tries to skip in the squares, but has to support himself on the other leg each time, pissed. When he bends down to pick up his keys, her hand is quicker than his.

She walks in: into what is no longer there, he thinks, as he stands there on one leg in square five. He's listening to how she's running from room to room, up the stairs, down the stairs. He's thinking about the clothes he's cut to pieces, *Für Elise* in smithereens. Then he starts skipping again, back and forth across the squares, until he's throwing up. Finally he notices the heavy silence, almost like a scream.

—Nusch, he calls, frightened, and runs after her, in through the door, through the whole house, until he finds her in front of the wardrobe in the bedroom, mute. Together they look at the empty shelves, the empty drawers, the hat shelf with the cutup wigs, the naked hangers. Only his clothes are hanging there now. And the bed has the same bedding it did the day she left. Flowery, bloodstained. They stand for a while, studying it all, as if it was a crime scene. Then she pulls him with her, into the living room. In the corner where the piano stood, there's only the phone book. He doesn't know what to say. He hadn't expected this moment. Did he really believe that he'd never see her again? Still, without being totally aware of it himself, his lips begin to move, make sounds. Alarmed, he can hear himself saying that he packed all her clothes and sent them to poor children in

Bosnia. He claims that he was attracted by the idea that their grief could be of some good to others. His cheeks become warm as he keeps talking. She torments him for a long time with her silence. Then she starts to laugh. She can't believe that he'd do something so childish.

—But the piano? she says after a while.

—You don't need that anymore.

She doesn't know what to say, just stands there openmouthed. Her laughter has gotten stuck.

—The piano, she repeats, like an echo, her voice cracking, untuned. Surely that doesn't fit in a box?

—Fuck the piano, he says, stroking her tense shoulder. You'll never need to play it anymore, not ever.

She leans her head against his chest. Then she takes off her yellow shawl and shows him the uneven, half-long hair that's also getting shorter and shorter. It looks hopeless, but it suits her. He grabs her bony, determined hand, leads her quickly past the closet and into the bathroom. There he finds the scissors, the ones he used on himself, on the clothes, the wig. He begins to cut off the uneven patches of her red hair, cuts and cuts, until she sits in front of him with a boy's hair style.

She wants to see how she looks, but there's no longer a mirror in this house. Instead, he shows her his hands full of scars; he claims that when she left, all he could see in the mirror was her absence. She looks at him sadly, but he says no, that's not necessary. Instead, he thanks her for everything he gets to experience. All this preciously experienced pain that only she can give him. He seems almost proud as he leaves her. She sits there alone just for a moment, because he soon comes back. In his hands he holds a polished saucepan. She looks surprised as he holds it up in the air. Then her face appears in the pot, distorted, as in a Tivoli mirror. Her head looks as round as a ball or perhaps an apple, he thinks, and her newly cut hair looks like a hedgehog. She laughs a little at her image: she doesn't recognize herself, and he laughs with her. But when she asks if he wants to look at himself in the saucepan too, he just shakes his head.

When a woman leaves a man, he cuts his hair to forget her. When a woman loses her mind, she cuts her hair to prove that she has really gone mad. When a man cuts the hair of the woman he loves, it's to forget that he has lost his mind and taken her back—even though she has left him many times, and will perhaps leave him again.

He can't remember when they went to bed, how they ended up in bed or if they made love. Just that he woke up with a hangover, naked, next to her, in this suspended state where you can't do anything, your head hurts, and you end up staying in bed, eating junk food and watching film after film until you fall asleep again.

They don't do a lot the first few days, but that doesn't matter. To be together is enough, in the beginning.

Mornings alone:

They sleep well at night, either spooning or with their arms wrapped around each other. But in the mornings, she can feel that itch again somewhere inside her. Not exactly on the skin, but beneath it. She can't quite get to it. That's why she gets up early, without waking him. She keeps strictly to her morning routine. Without it, she'll let herself deteriorate. It involves putting her hand in the coffee container, preparing the coffeemaker, filling the flat with this bitter smell, doing fifty sit-ups and twenty pushups, washing the dishes if there are some left from the night before. Then she takes the kitchen stool into the living room, where the piano was. Just sits there and stares at the phone book, or out the window, where the hopscotch was. After a while she puts the kitchen stool back in the kitchen, empties the coffeemaker in the sink and takes out an ice cube from the freezer. She uses the ice cube to wash her face so that the makeup will keep during the day. There are still no mirrors in this house, she thinks with irritation, but she doesn't do anything about it, doesn't buy a new one: morning after morning. Instead, she continues to use the saucepan, and if that's dirty, a spoon, a knife, or a fork. She's become so used to the comic effect by now that it's stopped having an impact on her. She concentrates on making dark outlines in the waterlines, draws her eyebrows and darkens her eyelashes. She hides her freckles with a thick layer of powder. She needs to hide away in this thing called Nusch which he, strangely enough, has fallen in love with. She's only herself in the morning, when he's asleep and she can wander around in her own, strict world. Like how you must practice impossible notes, she repeats again and again: life.

She looks at her watch: twelve. About the time she usually begins to miss him. She puts away her makeup, puts the kettle back on the hotplate, puts the cutlery in the drawer, takes a pill, maybe two, and sneaks into the bedroom again. Stands in the middle of the room for a while, looking at him lying on his side, all by himself. There's something in his unaware loneliness that touches her. She takes off her dressing gown, carefully hangs it back up in the wardrobe, and lies down on her side too, close to his body. She lies like that for a long time, pretending to sleep: quiet, stiff, staring at the wall with a thick, heavy layer of mascara on her eyelashes. Finally she closes her eyes without being aware of it herself.

Mornings together:

He wakes up with her body glued to his. Her sleeping face is unnatural, unreal, like that of a wax doll. He prods her discretely. She opens her eyes, looks at him from beneath her eye shadow.

—The worst thing about two people finding each other again, is that they might lose each other again, he says.

She says nothing to that. Yawns lightly, stretches. He looks down on her naked, goose-pimpled body. Studies her skinny bum, her thin thighs with scratches from his long nails, and says he doesn't quite know how to explain it, because it isn't just that he becomes so enormously horny when he's thinking about these body parts of hers; he feels happy as well. He asks if she can understand that. She shakes her head, holds her crotch, and says she has to pee. He follows, his prick raised. She turns to him, admits that she's probably less unhappy with him than without him. Which doesn't mean that she's happy, just less discontent.

After she's used the bathroom, they make love again.

She's the type that's never quite happy, always a bit nervous—and with stomach problems. When she goes to the toilet, she can't quite empty her bladder, but has to go again and again. He says it's psychosomatic. That no one needs to go that often. That it isn't normal. She says he's right, but she can't do anything about it, she's too weak. He doesn't agree. Says her biggest weakness is that she believes she's weak. Claims instead that she must be strong: with so much self-contempt and hate inside of her, she can't be anything else. He's attracted to all she's been through, he then says, almost a bit ashamed. Admits it's a strange form of perversion. That what he first noticed was her lack of enthusiasm. That her eyes were so vacant and expressionless. That her body was so fragile. But he knows that to let oneself deteriorate in such a sophisticated and precise way as she does, you have to be strong-willed and disciplined. That's what he's afraid of.

He opens the wardrobe. They look at his clothes together, and the wig. She takes a long time to decide. Finally, she dresses in his turquoise y-fronts, white singlet, checked work shirt, and much-too-big jeans that she tightens with a leather belt. He dresses almost the same. They look at each other and smile at their similar outfits.

She makes the coffee while he gets the breakfast. That's how they do it. He takes great care: scrambled eggs, bacon, sausages. But she usually just picks at her food. He notices how she fights to stay awake, how her eyelids close and open, how her head makes an effort not to fall forward. He wonders why she needs so much sleep. She stays sitting up, sipping her coffee while he's reading the local and international papers, reading everything carefully, every word, every sentence. Now and then he looks up at her and smiles, breadcrumbs in the corners of his mouth. He tells her what's in the employment notices. And about what's happening around the world. Natural disasters, wars. But she isn't paying attention. Honestly, she isn't.

—What do you want to do today? she asks instead.

He shrugs his shoulders.

Afternoons:

They go for a walk. Past the hopscotch that isn't there anymore. Up the hill, and then quickly past the garbage dump's sweet, somewhat nauseating odor. He walks in front, while she tags along absentmindedly. They're not walking to get somewhere—that's why she can't understand why he's in such a hurry. They walk in order to walk. To be together, she thinks, and gives herself ample time: she looks at her reflections in his sunglasses, but also in the windows of random cars and the dirty windows in the blocks of flats.

Evenings:

While they're lying in bed watching a French film, she tells him about the place she used to live. Before she met him. He's heard the story many times before, but he doesn't stop her. Instead, he listens to her as if he's hearing it for the first time. She describes how dark it was. Pitch dark. No difference between night and day. Everything was night. She admits that she misses this darkness. That it made her feel safe.

As soon as the film has finished, they put on another one.

Such are their days. It's better to be bored together than to be bored alone, she thinks. You are less bored when you're bored with someone, knowing that the other one's just as bored, he thinks.

There's something he's forgotten about Nusch. Something essential, he suspects, something that defines her as a person. No matter how trivial it might be, the thing he's forgotten, he can't forget that he's forgotten it. And he thinks about it even more. That which he doesn't know.

The months pass. Clothes are being bought, clothes that become worn, lose their shape. New memories are created: memories that soon become like the old ones. The box room remains locked. They're more and more often invited to dinner parties with friends they don't care about, and who don't care about them either. But couples meet other couples. That's life.

One night they're at dinner at a friends' place, Nusch sits down at the piano in their living room. She sits there for ages; no one notices, except him. Their friends continue to talk. Only he feels the intense suspense. But no sounds come from the piano, not a single one. He runs over to her, sees that she's crying. That she has dug her nails into the palms of her hands. That she's grinding her teeth. He doesn't know what to do, tries to tickle her a little. But she tightens her muscles even more. Their friends still don't notice anything, instead they put on an old record and start dancing. He observes how they move: shaking their hands, boobs, bottoms. The floor almost quivers beneath them. It suddenly strikes him how fat they've all become, as compared to Nusch. He looks at her again, at this swollen face that he's been missing. Then he dries her tears with the sleeve of his sweater. They're dirty, with small puddles of black eyeliner. He notices that the corners of her mouth are twitching. Perhaps she wants to laugh, he thinks, relieved. He listens, but there's no sound now either. Perhaps she didn't really want to after all. Suddenly she knocks the piano lid over one of her hands. A dreadful noise. And then silence. He looks at her with fearful eyes. Their friends have stopped dancing. He pulls her discretely out into the hallway. Makes their excuses, sorry but they have to leave. Walk fast. Run.

Once at home, he asks her to scream. He's read in an old

women's magazine that it can help against this sort of thing. She begins carefully, shyly, and then she tries a little more, and then she lets go. But it doesn't calm her down, rather the opposite: the more she screams, the more hysterical she becomes. Bites his lower lip and asks him to squeeze her crotch. Asks him to squeeze hard. Harder. Wants it to show.

Still nothing changes. Ostensibly.

But afterward, Nusch begins to get up even earlier. When the streetlamps are still lit. And the steps in her routine increase, become more and more demanding, stricter. Now and then she stops and observes herself from the outside: how she wanders around the house dealing with trifles. She still keeps doing it. Sits down on the kitchen stool in the living room. But while before she would only sit there and stare out of the window, or at the phone book, now she picks it up and lays it on her lap. Leafs through it as if it were a sheet of notes, as if she were trying to find *Für Elise*. After a while she puts the phone book back on the floor. Removes all traces. Takes her pills, often two now, maybe three. Then she walks into the bedroom and spoons him.

It becomes increasingly difficult for him to get her out of bed. When they finally get up, Nusch makes the coffee as always while he makes the breakfast. That's how it is. But these days she often forgets to put water in the percolator or coffee in the filter. She doesn't pay attention and has to start again and again. And when breakfast is ready, she doesn't pick at her food anymore; she pretends it isn't there. And he pretends not to notice how thin she's become. She's almost one with the chair, the wallpaper, the floor. Instead of saying anything, he hides behind the newspapers.

He thinks to himself that they have to do something with their lives, but doesn't quite know what, or how. They could at least get a dog, he suggests one day. Pee, go for walks, feed, cuddle? But she says she's allergic to everything with fur. He tries to think of other things they can do together. Gives up. Perhaps he lacks imagination. Now and then he ruffles her boy-hair that's grown long down the neck now, almost like a mullet. Tries to push into her. Occasionally he makes it, is allowed to, at other times she's quite simply too tired to open up. He's scared that she'll disappear into her own world altogether and forget him again.

They cling to each other, cling together. Persevere.

One morning he turns around in bed, wriggles closer and closer to where he believes she's lying, until he falls out. He stands up, confused, looks for her under the duvet, but she's gone. Afraid, he runs into the hallway, then suddenly stops, as he discovers her sitting on a stool in the living room, where her piano was. He breathes a sigh of relief. Until he sees how she moves her fingers in the air, as if looking for the keys. Now and then she stops, bends forward and studies the phone book. Leafs through it, as if it were sheets of music, as if she has played a false note. For a moment, she turns her head toward where he's hiding behind the door, but without noticing that he's there. It's been a long time since he's seen her totally without makeup. Her face is full of perspiration. She dries it with a napkin.

Then he walks slowly back to the bedroom, without making a single sound. Lies down in bed again and pretends to be asleep.

He wasn't meant to see that, he thinks, so he never mentions it to anyone. Not even to Nusch.

Repercussions:

While he used to throw himself at her and tear off her clothes, he has now lost some of that spontaneity. In a strange way, he has become meticulous and takes her clothes off slowly, almost sophisticatedly. He folds them together, makes the bed, and crawls under the duvet. Sometimes they make love, but usually not.

He disappears into his memories, into what's no longer there. These are the things he thinks about: how she always stood alone in a corner in high school, until he came and stood there with her. Then they became infatuated. Tied a bond. With a knot that slowly became so tight that it almost strangled her. And that's the way it was. Because she told him that.

Sometimes he stands and stares at the same wall for hours on end. Then she'll ask him what he's thinking of, and he just shrugs his shoulders and answers: nothing. But in his head the same picture always appears: a deserted landscape where everything is dead. Where all the flowers have withered, and nothing can grow. She walks ahead and he moseys behind.

The blind eye:

During one of the many breakfasts, he notices that she has exchanged her cutlery for scissors.

—What's the alternative to being together, she asks, while she makes hole after hole in his leather belt.

—To be alone, he answers and is silent for a long time. Chews his sausages, bacon.

She doesn't say anything, just continues to make holes. Tiny round pieces of leather fall on her plate.

Finally, she leaves the table even if he hasn't finished eating. Throws her food discretely, or perhaps rather demonstratively, in the bin. He's not quite sure.

Nusch changes a bit every day. It's almost imperceptible, but it does happen. Her waist slowly but surely adjusting to the new holes in his leather belt. Her hair growing longer and longer down her neck, plaited in a rattail. Her nails becoming pointed, her eyes becoming pointed as well. Soon he no longer recognizes her.

He clings on, keeps clinging on. She lets go.

One night he wakes up to a terrible racket. He looks out of the crack in the curtain. Sees several garbage bins that have toppled over and a fox running away with a bent, disposable grill in its mouth. He turns towards Nusch, realizes she's not there. He sneaks out of bed, quietly, out of the room, through the hallway, into the living room, into the kitchen, the bathroom, up the stairs, down the stairs, quickly past the box room. He can't find her anywhere. Just these tiny pieces of leather from his belt lying spread across the kitchen table. He picks them up, one by one. Holds them in his hand. They remind him of cutoff moles.

He throws them away, begins madly running around the house, back and forth through all the rooms, again and again.

—Nusch! he calls. Nusch!

But the only answer he gets is his own breath.

The makeup, her yellow shawl, and his wig are all gone. Other than that, she's taken nothing with her, as far as he can see.

He doesn't know what to do. Stands still in the middle of the living room for a long time, then he goes into the kitchen and makes coffee. Tired, he sits down with his cup and decides to begin the long, excruciating wait for her to come back. Yet again. That's all he's equipped for. It's vital to keep calm until she's home again. Not lose his cool like last time. Calmly wait. Cut his nails, not his hair, weed the flowerbeds, water the plants, make them grow again: these feelings he's sure he has for her, must have had. He looks at the empty space where the piano once stood. Looks at the phone book, intensely, questioningly, looking for answers.

He goes out a few hours later, takes a piece of chalk from his pocket, and redraws the lines of hopscotch squares where he thinks they used to be. Puts the toppled garbage bins back in place, picks up ice cream paper, a swimming ring, ketchup bottles, a disposable camera, a freezer bag, and puts it all in the back of his rusty car. As always, he drives irresponsibly fast up the hill toward the garbage dump, throws it all in there. He just wants something to do. In the pile of rubbish, he finds some of his old porno magazines. He wipes some moldy sauce off the pages and takes them home with him.

When he comes back, the house is still empty.

Hibernation:

To make time pass, he hangs from his legs: a hook around his foot and a bar from the doorframe, his head turned down like a bat's. His pulse sinks, like his body temperature. He tries to rest that way. But all that happens is that he gets a headache.

He stands up, lies down in bed, puts on her favorite film: *L'ennui*. Watches it again and again, until it gets stuck.

This only happens without Nusch, that he feels the days are too long. When two weeks have passed without a sign from her, he thinks that perhaps he should get a job. He imagines the different things he can do with the money he'll soon earn. Falls into dreams. The best idea, he thinks, is to take her with him to the Mediterranean or something. He reads catalogues from travel bureaus that may no longer exist, that may well have gone bankrupt. Puts a cross on the pages that interest him. But then he changes his mind, suddenly thinks of her skin, as white as chalk beneath the hot Mediterranean sun: sunburned, scorched.

Mornings alone:

One morning as he sits and picks at his breakfast, he reads an article that catches his attention. It says that people with red hair have a higher pain threshold than others because they have a mutation in a certain gene. And this gene causes their hair to be red, their skin to be pale, and their tolerance for pain to be higher than the rest of the population's. He closes the paper, throws the food in the bin, and wonders if that's why it takes her so long to come back.

A few hours later, as he stands and looks out of the dirty window, a black bird flies past. There's nothing strange about that, he thinks, but as it passes the row of rusted cars, something falls out of its mouth. Curious, and with nothing better to do, he runs out. He finds a white piano string on the footpath. In two pieces. Ecstatic, he runs back in. Eagerly, he glues it together, puts it carefully in a worn shoebox, and lights a couple of candles.

He spends the next few days washing the windows, ironing his shirts, cutting his nails, and making an appointment with the hairdresser. He must have a proper haircut this time: straight across the neck, the way she likes it.

He thinks about new things to do every day. He weeds the flowerbeds, secures the cement tiles that have fallen from the exterior walls of the house, buys dresses for her, and hangs up a new mirror in the bathroom. She won't want for a thing this time.

He keeps going like that for weeks.

One day, when he's washing the mirror in the bathroom, he stops and watches himself nervously, in small glimpses. There's something strange in his eyes, something faded. It's as if all the tears have watered them out and made them light, light blue, almost white. It frightens him, and he looks down. Feels that he is slowly but surely losing his individuality. That he's beginning to resemble her, more and more. Not unhappy, but not quite happy either. The condition he used to find so attractive in her, he now dislikes immensely in himself.

But even without Nusch, time passes inexplicably: summer, autumn, winter, and spring. He had a job for a short time, as a postman, but he soon lost it because he constantly forgot to deliver the letters. They piled up in his living room. He opened them carefully with steam from a kettle. None of them was from her. To him.

He tells himself that it's a choice. That loneliness is a choice. That there always comes a point when you can choose. He thinks that it's better to be depressed than bored. At least you're experiencing something then. He admits that in a strange way, the worst moments of his life are also the most beautiful.

Sleepwalker:

Sometimes he moves cautiously outside the house. Walks through the streets at night. Promenades. But he never walks in any kind of direction. He walks in order to walk, that's all. To move his legs. Now and then he throws pebbles at the streetlights. Watches as the lights go out, one by one. He begins to understand it now, this darkness she talked about.

One day, as he stands inside staring out, a white bird flies straight into one of the newly washed windows. He runs out, picks it up. It looks at him with its marble-round eyes. Still warm. He holds it in his hand, holds his breath. He doesn't know what comes over him, but suddenly he breaks the bird's wing. The sound is beautiful, like autumn, like stepping on a withered branch.

As he's about to go back in, he notices the old woman in the house opposite staring at him. He throws the bird in the bin and walks over to the house across the street. Before he can ring the doorbell, she comes out on the stoop dressed in men's striped pajamas. She asks with a hopeful and frail voice if he has seen her husband. He shakes his head. Then she asks him to come inside and wait with her for a while. She says she's afraid of being alone. Afraid that strange men should force their way into her house and do terrible things to her.

He leaves his shoes in the hallway, stands there waiting while the old woman fetches a pair of worn men's slippers. He is a bit taken aback, but he puts them on. They're a perfect fit. There's a platter of Brown Betties with whipped cream on the table. The old woman tells him to help himself. His plate is already on the table, as if she's been waiting for him. A few breadcrumbs fall off the top. The old woman brushes the morsels onto the carpet. Her hands are large and sturdy, almost those of a worker, he thinks. He sits deep in her armchair and lights cigarette after cigarette, which she puts in front of him even though he doesn't smoke. They belong to her husband, she explains. He smiles gratefully, puts out the cigarette. Then he finally picks up the courage and asks her how longs she's been waiting.

—It's been a few years now. Were you in Dresden during the bombing? she asks in a quavering voice.

He suddenly feels how the nicotine is stinging his throat. He stands up without having touched the dessert, looks at his watch, says he has something important to do, puts on his shoes, and runs across the street.

Back at home, he stands for a long time and looks around the house. I can't become like her, he thinks, and tries to think of something important he can do, something factual. Something he can hold on to. He feels he's becoming dizzy. Goes to fetch the kitchen stool. Puts in it the living room where the piano used to be. Stands and stares at the phone book for a while, as if to compose himself. Then he begins to leaf through it. Reads names, addresses and phone numbers. Reads each letter and each single figure carefully. Until he suddenly stops.

Piperno, László, Atomveien 22 B 35 95 00 81

He drags his finger many times across the letters. Reads them again and again. It's the first time he's seen his name in print. Really seen it. He thinks it sounds great. He's never thought about it like that before, with a chime. He slides his finger down the page, looking for her name, for Nusch Piperno. While he does, sweat is trickling down his forehead. He dries it with a napkin. Can't find her name anywhere. Instead, he stumbles across names of people he's almost forgotten and who are certain to have forgotten him too. People who used to be his friends, people he used to visit and who'd visit him. A girlfriend from primary school. Even the name of the firm of his previous job is listed here in the phone book, with number, address, everything. He turns back a few pages and looks at his name again.

Everything in this house belongs to me, he then thinks, almost surprised, and puts down the phone book. There are no traces of Nusch anywhere—not in the kitchen, the bathroom, nor the bedroom. Except in the closet. He doesn't know what comes over him, but he finds the key he's been hiding for such a long time. It surprises him how small it looks in the palm of his hand. He draws a deep breath, walks over to the closet and turns the key.

The sun is illuminating the small room through an oval window. Carefully, he lets his eyes roam from corner to corner, but he can't make sense of anything he sees. He tries once again. Puzzled. From corner to corner, and then toward the middle. But it doesn't change anything. The closet is and remains empty.

Thank you to Marco Demian Vitanza, Ådel Odilon, Noise and Noisette, Trude Rønnestad, Hanne Ramsdal, Nikolaj Frobenius, Hilde Stubhaug, Irene Engelstad and all those who helped me when my text was coming apart.

Edy Poppy (b. 1975), grew up on a farm in Bø, Telemark, Norway. She moved to Montpellier when she was 17, and spent several years in France before moving to London where she worked with art, fashion, film and writing. She is the author of the novel Anatomy.Monotony., which has been translated into Italian, Finnish, German, Polish and English, as well as the short story collection Coming. Apart. and most recently the novel IGGY. Poppy has lived in Berlin, Buenos Aires, Lipari, Reykjavik, and Rio, and now calls Norway home once again, living in Oslo.

May-Brit Akerholt's published translations of Norwegian works include plays, novels, and poetry collections by writers such as Henrik Ibsen, Jon Fosse, and Ruth Lillegraven. She lives in Australia, where she is a recipient of a fellowship from the Theatre Board of Australia Council.

www.ingramcontent.com/pod-product-compliance
Lightning Source LLC
Jackson TN
JSHW081434180825
89174JS00001B/1
* 9 7 8 1 6 2 8 9 7 6 2 8 1 *